The Real, True Angel

stories by

Robin Lippincott

february 1997

for Enid,

i the thanks and

best wishes.

Robin

Fleur-de-Lis Press / Louisville, Kentucky

Library of Congress Catalog Card Number: 96-84722
ISBN: 0-9652520-0-0
Copyright © 1996 by Robin Lippincott
first printing, August 1996

Printed in U.S.A. by University of Louisville Printing and Publications.

Published by The Louisville Review Corporation, 312D Bingham
Humanities, University of Louisville, Louisville, KY 40292

The Real, True Angel

for Lee

Acknowledgments

Apalachee Quarterly, "Five O'clock Shadow"
Christopher Street, "Forcing Forsythia"
Crosscurrents, "The 'I' Rejected"
The Louisville Review, "Idyll of My Son," and "If You're Going to San Francisco"
Provincetown Arts, "The Real, True Angel"

My heartfelt thanks to the following people: my sisters and co-conspirators, Marcia Kay Lippincott and Cindy Brown, and my parents, Robert W. and Marcia L. Lippincott; Michael Anderson at *The New York Times Book Review*, Bruce Aufhmammer, Ellen Balber, Steve Bauer and Suzanne Marcus, the late Walta Borawski, Dr. Lawrence Borges, Christoper Busa at *Provincetown Arts*, Hortensia Cardona, Martha and Rodri Corazon, Mary Lee Fowler, Jennifer Hagar, Anne Hoppe, Lois Hurst, Sharon Ivanhoe, Michael Jakubisin, Eugene Kaelin, Ellen Lesser and Roger Weingarten, Karen J. Mann, Stephen McCauley, Sena Jeter Naslund (mentor-extraordinaire), Bob and Carol O'Handley, Gerrie Paino, Frankie Paino (for her passionate example), Rick Reinkraut, the late Ilyana Reiser, Louise Riemer, Sheila Ortiz Taylor, and Kirkby Tittle.

Contents

"The 'I' Rejected"

was what she wrote toward the end, what she wrote she wanted to achieve in what would, though she did not know it then, be her last book; and in her life, too, I think. And she did, both in the novel and in her death by drowning, did achieve it, so floats amongst us now a "we," as she stood beside me that spring afternoon and knelt by the pond (two years before her death), knelt that day in 1939, folded that long, elegant body of hers to examine an "emerald" frog on a lily pad and saw her reflection as a breeze rippled the water's surface; saw herself as she now appears amongst us. "There she is," she said to me, pointing at her own reflection and referring to herself in the third person, "the phantom"; and then she laughed that big, whooping laugh of hers, laughed and said soberly, "I am dispersed," and smiled at me wistfully. And it was after that, that she muttered to herself, turning away, not meaning, I'm sure, for me to hear, muttered: "The only way." That was the last time I saw her.

*

Who am I? The I of me—my name? I shall remain nameless. Call me anonymous. I, too, am a phantom, a ghostly apparition, an old man almost transparent now in my twilit days; one so terribly lonely.

Then, in 1939, when I was twenty-four, an only child whose parents had recently died, then I was one of several, a "we" of several young men from Oxford, etc., one of a few who, in various and roundabout ways, through Spender and Isherwood and perhaps less so Auden, one of a few drawn into her circle. I saw her perhaps only ten times over the years, but knew her well enough to know, for example, that she liked her coffee black and strong; liked good food with plenty of salt; liked good talk, and liked, of course, her special cigarettes, which she and her husband would roll of an evening. I knew her well enough, too, not to delude myself, and to admit that the way to know her best, to be closest to her, no surprise, was through her work. And so I read and reread and have recently reread again, everything she published.

My name is not to be found in any of the published diaries or letters, or in any of the many published accounts of that group, that time, that place. Because I, after all, am a homosexual, and we have often remained anonymous throughout history; a gay man, as they say today, a usage I strongly dislike, and at which she, I'm sure, would have been absolutely horrified. "The bastardization of the English language!" I can just hear her saying it in that teasing, sonorous voice she had. Of course there were homosexuals in her own group of friends, "buggers" they were called; her circle was known for them. But they were all distinguished: Strachey, before my time; Keynes; Morgan Forster and so on, through Isherwood, whom I knew, of course, etc. The individual could distinguish himself from the pack, but I did not. Not then. I was just another "bugger."

She was a very personal person, you see, an individualist (quite the opposite of her husband), and had sought, for most of her life, to distinguish herself in a *very* distinguished family and group of friends, which of course she did. *Enormously.* Perhaps *most* successfully. At a price.

*

It happens to all of us upon occasion, I suspect, riding on the tube one sees a face on the body opposite one thinks is his own. His hand reflexes up to his face; a stroke, a brush, to feel if he is still there; and then one almost reaches out to the face across, so intense and symbiotic is the feeling. He begins to wonder if he is himself after all. And if not, who?

Riding the tube is my daily constitutional, only yesterday there was no one sitting opposite me, and the face I saw reflected in the glass, on my body, was hers. I am now, in old age, rather pink and pinched, as she was late in her life, that which can still be beautiful on a woman but not on a man; but this was her face, her features, and not my own. Gave me such a fright, good lord!

I arrived home that afternoon, I have lived in this same flat in Leicester Square for over twenty years, arrived home feeling all helter-skelter, so I made a pot of tea and sat in the dying light of the day still feeling shaken; feeling as though I'd lost all sense of myself. Too much time alone, no doubt, I thought, so I rang up Maggie, whom I've known as many years as I taught at the university, some thirty-odd, and dear, inelegant Maggie, a colleague's secretary all those years, an old maid, Maggie, who doesn't really know me at all, nor I her, said, "Do let's meet for supper then," and so we did, and had a good hoot, and afterwards I felt restored, myself again, and came home, put on my smoking jacket, poured myself a brandy, and a nip in old Tom's bowl, then sat before the fire warming and looking at my hands in the light, and thinking.

*

I did not mean to suggest earlier, in mentioning that spring afternoon in 1939 as the two of us knelt by the pond, did not by any means mean to suggest that the event and what she said that day was at all premonitory or ominous, or that I somehow knew. Not at all. In fact, there is such a volume of water in her work and in her life; it was commonplace. But I must admit I was not surprised when I heard how she did it, or that she had done it at all, really. (I remember a biographer pointing out that one of her earliest memories was of her mother, and of the water outside her window. The biographer wrote, ending the book I believe, and I paraphrase: in her beginning was her end. Smashing, to achieve such symmetry!)

Look, for example, at the work: her first novel is set at sea; the third begins on a beach; the fifth and some think finest, set on an island. There is a fluidity in her best work, a rushing liquescence which, when not present, as in that flat second book, makes the work seem grounded. And in my favorite, each chapter begins with a description of the ocean at a later, ever-darkening time of day. Then there is the last, that dark, haunted pool of a book, about which my friend John Lehmann showed me shortly after her death, (from a letter she had written him):

> "If I live another 50 years I think I shall put this method to use, but as in 50 years I shall be under the pond, with the goldfish swimming over me. . . ."

In that last, unfinished, beautiful book, a work I have always thought of, and taught, as capturing, and perhaps prophesying, the atomization that the Second War brought to the world, and that she herself felt so keenly, living in London and Rodmell in her last years and days. In the last book, this is her reference to that pond:

"It was in that deep center, in that black heart, that the lady had drowned herself."

*

If I go to a club, which I do now very rarely, but if I do go to a club, I am ignored, and may as well be nonexistent, invisible. Oh, I get waited on all right. "Scotch on the rocks," I'll say to the inevitably blonde boy behind the bar. The drink then gets plopped down and splashes onto the counter, I hand him money, say "keep the change," he smiles, and that is the extent of any intercourse. Occasionally I'll see other older men there who look at me as if they despise me, because I remind them of themselves, I think, and because they probably figure one old man, for the chance fetishist, is enough, has better odds. The music is too loud and the smoke too thick, but what I enjoy, what I go for, besides looking, is the smell; yes, that sense is still vibrant: sweat and aftershave and cologne (there's a difference) and poppers, (poppers were common even back in the Fifties), and urine, and even sex, yes, for there is a back room. But then always when I leave I am haunted by my own terrible self-consciousness as I see myself reflected in the glass door on my way out. I walk home to an almost empty flat, Tom brushes against my pants leg, and I sit down before a fire and review my life, which only lends itself to

sleepless nights, regrets, recriminations, and resolutions to
end the terrible loneliness.

*

Roland Barthes died, was killed rather, and rather
absurdly I must say, struck down by a van as he was
crossing the street, on his way to post a letter, in Paris. I
have always thought she would have appreciated his work.
And the two of them do rather look alike. Perhaps what set
this whole remembering engine running, besides the dark
pressing of my last days, was my reading, several weeks
back, that Barthes—toward the end of his life (which he did
not know, of course, to be the end)—had come to the end of
something in his work, and that he felt the "I" had to be
"dismantled." Barthes is, in fact, quoted as having said, or
written, that "True knowledge depends upon the unmasking
of the 'I'." At which point she, the author of the piece on
Barthes, a noted American intellectual, wrote: ". . . the great
project of depersonalization which is the aesthete's highest
gesture of good taste."

*

I, myself, sit in my flat. Retired now. A Chair at the
University; an office, where I can go if I choose, which I
don't: I am tired. I sit in my flat by the fire and stare at my
hands against the light. I am so terribly lonely. I never did
find another, a man with whom to share my life. Oh, there
were trysts here and there that became more desperate, more
depraved, as I grew older, but never did I find a mate: the
great sadness of my life.

Yes, I am tired. Tired of academic life, tired of books
and theories and arguments and abstractions; tired, yes, let

it be said, of myself. Odd: one might think I would associate her with all that, but I do not. Instead, I remember her laugh and her conversational flights: she was a fun person to be with, and took one places, if one happened to be sitting next to her at the time, included one in those fanciful flights of the mind.

*

Birds singing; green leaves, green grass, and a border of brush, darker green, lush, around the pond; sky and pond surface blue, periwinkle blue, and the light, soft; a slight breeze, a shimmering of leaves and of the water's surface, yes spring!; the rubbing together, almost whistle, of her brown jersey skirt and long jacket, as we walk along, the group of others fading in the distance behind us; the juices of the grass staining her suede shoes as she steps, sending a sweet, pungent scent up, up, up; but then suddenly, as we near the pond, before she kneels and spots the frog, (yes between this and the moment she knelt, there had to be a long interlude in which I "explained" myself), she says, "I get no sense of you at all. Do tell me about yourself."

*

And so whether it was then, in the spring of 1939, when she knelt down beside me at the edge of the pond; or a few days ago when she visited me on the tube; or years from now, when I am dead, in a new century, when she lights on the streets of London in a simple shop girl; she is now and forever a "we," a "we" of me, of you, of us all.

And so now "I" will leave my flat one day soon and walk out into the busy streets of London, walk out into the rush of traffic; of the Queen, perhaps, passing by, caught, temporarily, in a traffic jam; of angry, nihilistic, spike-haired youngsters; of the bobby mounted on a horse oblivious to all, including his horse's droppings, as he talks to a crony on the street corner; will walk out and fling myself ("the only way") against all humanity, the parade, and thus become less myself, more a part of the whole, and finally not alone, yes!

Negative Capability

"Her eye," someone had once written, "is like a razor, like an envelope," and Zee had been pleased. But that was a few years ago; these days she rarely left her apartment.

Today, though, a balmy Saturday, just after sunrise, she stood in Washington Square Park staring at her black shoes and her body foreshortened against the sidewalk, an all-too-familiar vantage point. She recalled the image of herself she had seen in a storefront window moments before: a pale, slim, figure with short dark hair and bad teeth, wearing a black, sleeveless jersey, black mini-skirt, and black stockings.

An hour earlier, oblivious to time, she had called her old friend Monroe Baker: "Jimmy," she'd nicknamed him nine years ago, a year after they'd met. She asked Jimmy if she could stop by. Surprised to hear she'd awakened him, she said it had been a long time, too long; six months? But no, nothing was wrong. She was trying to sound casual.

"Of course, Zee, darling," Jimmy said. She imagined him sitting up in bed, naked, wiping a hand across his smooth, sleep-slack face and over his spiky crewcut. "You're the one person I'd love to see!"

Zee shuddered now, thinking of Jimmy's soft, brown, doe-like eyes, his dimples and his sly smile.

It was relatively quiet still for New York. There were a few other people out: a group of hippies, several with "Impeach Nixon" signs, dressed in bright, multicolored clothes sitting in a semicircle on the damp grass at one end of the park—like a rainbow—chanting; a bare-legged man in a raincoat (Zee wondered if he had anything on underneath) buying the morning paper from Eddie's newsstand on the corner. But most of the people she saw looked as if the park was their home: gray, rumpled, potatoey people, like in that painting of Van Gogh's. She yawned, looked up at the great arch, then down the row of browning, lifeless linden trees; it was early morning and there were no shadows, yet.

As she began walking, Zee felt a bump against her chest. She had forgotten. Hanging around her neck—she had to think about it now, as she had been thinking so often lately—was the fact of this rather large, square box that, for so many years, had preceded her everywhere she went: her weapon, her license, her shield. When she went out she put it on like other women put on lipstick, unconsciously, and it had become a part of her, like a wedding ring one could never take off without breaking the vow (she still wore hers). But now that she hadn't been going out, she hadn't picked it up, and so was more aware of it, and had begun to ask herself questions. This had been going on for a couple of months and was what had kept her from leaving the apartment.

Zee knew she had to get out, to see Jimmy, and had chosen this morning to face down her fears. She wore the camera now only to get to Jimmy's. But since she had to wear it, she had decided she would use the occasion to test herself, to see if she could make the walk without raising, or using, the camera *once*. It helped to know Jimmy was waiting for her. She would ponder these questions, she thought, *as she walked.*

Though not happy about it, Zee was living alone now, had been for a year, in an airy apartment on Charles Street. She talked to her two grown daughters—Lorna in Paris, Ariel across town—almost daily. Just last night she had spoken to Lorna, who'd told her that she was becoming aware of her animalism, feeling her wildness. Zee liked that. Lorna was mercurial. She looked like Zee had when she was Lorna's age: that sophisticated pout, the slight overbite and high cheekbones, her dark hair now cut in an elegant shag.

Lorna had been the first to leave home. She was seventeen, and neither Zee nor Orson had tried to stop her. That was eight years ago. Six years ago Zee and Orson had separated, permanently it turned out, against her wishes. Now he had remarried. And it was just last summer that, at twenty, Ariel—who more closely resembled Orson, was rounder in the face ("her dandelion," Zee had called her)—moved out.

Sometimes now, late at night, she would call Orson, still her best friend, in California, tell him she was scared. He was patient, tried to calm her, talked about their girls or suggested she invite a few friends over for her famous Hungarian goulash, the only dish she could make.

Yes, there were her friends, but they were, most of them, a part of what she was trying to get away from, what she called the scene: other photographers, artists, hangers-on; people whose motives she sometimes suspected and whose reasons for doing what they were doing she didn't always respect. Most were men, and Zee often felt patronized, felt they looked on her as something of an anomaly, a freak.

She had seen too much, that was it, so that—while only in her early forties—she felt old; tired; vanquished. She was overexposed.

Age was a part of it, too; she was losing her attrac-
tiveness. People had always commented on how youthful
she was, how, at thirty-nine, she'd looked twenty-nine. But
that had changed in the past few years. Overnight, it seemed.
Now, Zee noticed the lines parenthesizing her eyes and
gathering around her mouth; noticed, too, that men (and
women) were not drawn to her as they had once been.

She walked down Broadway, black dance shoes rhythmic
on the sidewalk. Her destination: "around 43rd and Broadway" was how she remembered it. The multitude of eager,
cheap storefronts and the bright colors of sidewalk sales
flashed and waved as she walked past. Peripheral to her
defiant eye, Zee resisted the primacy of one color over
another; all color; the easy. Instead, what she saw were
faces, faces, faces, faces; she was exploding with faces, all
stories, lives she couldn't contain but wanted to release into
some larger realm. (That was how it had been with Jimmy:
4'2", forty years old when they met ten years ago, married
twice to normal-sized women—his story showed on his
face).

In the beginning, when she first started out—coming
from a privileged upbringing—Zee had wanted to appropriate other lives, experience, as her own; to feel real. She
had grown up during the Depression feeling immune,
removed; she was told never to go near the men and women
in the bread lines on Fifth Avenue close to her father's
office (he was then a producer of Broadway shows). Zee
could remember standing and pressing her hands against her
bedroom window, looking out over Central Park from high
up and wanting to jump. Not to kill herself, but to be free.
Maybe they were the same thing. (Later, after she had
married young and moved out on her own, she would learn
the word for what she had felt: *alienated*). While in her early
teens she had tried to talk, really talk to her parents: her

mother, Xaviara, with her high forehead and Roman nose, so stately and imposing, chain-smoking, and her father, Daniel, slim and elegant, distant. Both of them looked at her as if she were from Mars. Everything, it seemed then, was forbidden, and for a long time since Zee had craved any and all experience, invited adversity, wanted to suffer. And she had done that.

During the years of commercial work with Orson, doing mostly fashion layouts, she would spend hours, sometimes days, on trivia—arranging a model's hair and make-up, coordinating the clothes, colors and props—while Orson took most of the pictures. She called herself a powder puff, and finally, after over ten years of working together, she and Orson agreed that she should set out on her own; he knew she was the more gifted. And in the seven years since she had seen and been through so much. Trying to develop her own style while hustling work for magazines to pay the bills. And then there were the pictures she'd started taking, the subjects. Most were depressing. She was tired, and worse, she felt she hadn't changed after all, or that she had changed completely, she wasn't sure which—had totally lost herself. But she couldn't stop, she had become the camera. And yet photography just didn't do it for her anymore, didn't thrill and titillate and move her as it once had. She likened it to a physical addiction where the addict needs greater and greater quantities of the drug—to the detriment of his health. Not taking pictures left a gaping hole in the center of her life.

Now, with the camera a weight around her neck, heavier on her mind, she would try not to look, would look down as she walked, watch her shoes slap the pavement, think of Jimmy, there, waiting; would listen to the rhythm, and remember.

Early on, she used to ride up and down the escalators at Macy's all afternoon to study the customer's faces. Faces held secrets. She remembered the glowing, mindless expressions on the faces at the first orgy she'd attended after Orson moved out; how terrified and nervous she had been, but how—with her camera—she felt brave, terrific. It had allowed her to do all kinds of things she never would have done alone, she knew.

How she'd wanted it, too, to lose herself. Just pin me down to the floor, she remembered thinking; pummel me; obliterate me. She had so longed to blend, to melt, to mold into all those other bodies and lives writhing around her; to be set free. It was the same feeling as her childhood love of swimming in the ocean: getting lost, swallowed up in that ancient and secret dark body. She had screamed for what seemed like minutes the first time she came with all those people, and for a while group sex had become another addiction.

She and Orson had had a good sex life, but Zee always felt she was missing out. There were so many different and distinctive ways to have sex, as many ways as there were people. Often men and women would look at her in the street, and afterwards, at home, she'd construct complex fantasies about them. But the fantasies only frustrated her; they were not the real thing: she was a powerless child again. Zee didn't need to fantasize about Jimmy; there had always been a powerful, almost frightening chemistry between them she knew would eventually surface, a chemistry that could possibly transform them both. With Jimmy she could just *be*.

Zee stepped off the curb to cross the street, heard the violent orange honk of a car horn and someone scream—at her? She looked up and saw the tense, angry face behind the windshield, the motioning hand, and stepped back onto the curb.

The street clear, only 24th, she crossed. A heavily made-up Latin woman clutching a small child passed by and looked at her as if she were crazy. Maybe it's the black clothes on a hot summer day, Zee thought, thinking, too, that she would always remember this face: caricature-thin eyebrows; thick, black eye-liner around brown eyes swimming in yellowy whites; red balls of blush on each cheek; fuchsia lipstick; and that black hair like wrought iron, framing the woman's triangular face. But all that was just a mask to her slightly turned-down mouth, her almost flaring nostrils, and her alert eyes, revealing pain and fright. Maybe she was new to the city. Zee resisted her impulse to shoot, looked down at her shoes hitting the pavement, and heard the rhythm was off.

The woman's face reminded her of the time she'd sat through twenty-four hours of Bergman films at the Bleecker Street Cinema. "For the brave at heart," the ad had read. "All masochists welcome." She considered herself neither, but went anyway, and sat, not following plot, but mesmerized, bewitched, by the faces. Bergman knew about faces as few contemporary artists did. He allowed the audience to watch as emotions slowly wash over the face, as the muscles move and change, shadows play, moment to moment. But his were all traditionally beautiful, almost aristocratic faces. Zee had other ideas about aristocracy, about what was beautiful.

She believed in existential courage, and she was a Romantic; believed that suffering was what ennobled, not money or birth. Not that suffering itself was beautiful, but that—if one survived it and had any character at all—one was deepened, made more human: like Jimmy.

Her daughters were both what most people thought of as beautiful, and Zee, though somewhat torn, took pride in that.

She had tried always not to protect or shield them too much, as she had been sheltered. She had let them go off on their own as much as possible, to wander, to risk. Once, at the West 13th Street playground with Ariel, Zee was sitting on a bench reading while Ariel played on a jungle-gym nearby. Another mother sitting next to her on the bench, noticing Zee's engrossment in her book, asked if she wasn't worried about her little girl. And though in that split-second after the woman's question and before her answer Zee had pictured Ariel's round face, a concentric circle around her mouth, open in a round "O" of pain, like Munch's "Scream," she had said no, that Ariel had to find out about life on her own, to take risks and, if necessary, get hurt.

She knew she had been a good mother, but if she had any faults—and she had overheard people say this—it was this leniency and lack of protection she offered. But her daughters seemed to have turned out all right; Orson thought so, too. She missed them now, walking along thinking of them, looking down—especially Lorna, in Paris, so far away.

Crossing the street she distinctly heard a third slapping sound, as if she were being closely followed by a one-legged man. She stopped, leaned against a streetlight and looked around, then down at her shoes. The heel of her left shoe was hanging loose, and as she lifted her foot, the heel came off in her hand, exposing a hole the size of a quarter. She would have to buy another pair, but she had no money with her. Her money situation hadn't been too good lately, especially since she hadn't been working. And her parents— whom she pictured now at their condo in Florida, where they'd retired, her mother more and more, with age, as her hairline receded, resembling George Washington, and her father shrunken and dried up from the sun, only his green eyes still vivid—had never helped out. She had brought only enough money to take the subway home, if she wanted to, if she couldn't stand being out any longer and wanted to get home fast. She took off the shoe and transferred it to her left hand; with the other shoe on her right foot, she figured, at least there would be a semblance of balance. She looked up: 36th Street. She had made it this far without raising her camera, but it didn't feel good.

What did give her pleasure was imagining Jimmy, now, in the hotel room where he had lived for over seventeen years, on the fourth floor overlooking a narrow, grimy alley on one side and a not much cleaner Broadway on the other. He had probably lain in bed for a while after her call, then gotten up, slipped into his dark paisley silk robe and padded barefoot into the kitchenette. On the phone he'd said he'd been asleep for a little over an hour when she called; it usually took him a while to unwind after a show, the last one ending around two in the morning.

She pictured him lighting a match to the gas jet as he put on water for coffee, then going into the bathroom, urinating, looking at his face in the make-up smudged mirror, and sitting down in his overstuffed, rose-colored chair waiting for the water to boil, waiting for her. This had been a long time coming, but Zee, though terrified, felt it was inevitable, necessary, and just hoped Jimmy felt the same. To give herself courage she remembered the day they met.

She had been watching him for two weeks. He always left his room at the hotel around four in the afternoon, and once again, as he had told her later, he saw her. As the sun hit his side of the street (it was March) and reflected off the revolving door of the hotel, it flashed on the black leather miniskirt she'd worn everyday. Black leather miniskirt, black turtleneck sweater, camera around her neck, everyday crouched there, at his level, tucked between two black-tiled buildings. For two weeks!

There had been no direct eye contact between them, but Jimmy said later he'd felt sure she was watching him; out of the corner of his eye he had seen her head turn as he walked down Broadway toward 43rd. He told her he had thought maybe she was one of those broads who gets off on doing it with freaks.

He had stalled in front of the hotel buttoning his coat. A button fell off, rolled and stopped in a crack in the sidewalk. (Later, he gave Zee the button as a souvenir of their first meeting.) He bent down and picked it up, lit a cigarette. He was on his way to work, said he should have been going over his lines for the show. He played Marilyn Monroe. There was a line he always skipped over: "Oh, just what they call interpretive dancing. You know, nightclubs."

Then—and Zee remembered this vividly—Jimmy had raised his fur-lined collar and pulled down the brim of his hat, as if preparing to make a move. But she stood up, and before he could take the first step, she crossed the street and was standing beside him.

"Hi," she had said, extending her hand, almost trembling, her voice high, girlish. "I saw you one day in Times Square and followed you home. I'd like to come up to your room. I'd like to photograph you, I mean, if you'd like that." And then she giggled. *That* was what had done it, Jimmy told her later (now he was pouring cream into his coffee): that giggle.

Zee stood across the street from Jimmy's hotel looking up at the window of his room. She'd arrived without taking a single picture, had passed the test. She lifted, and looked into her camera, snapped several shots of Jimmy's window—a blank eye hole—then lowered the camera in defeat. The effort, she thought, was like gratuitous sex with someone you'd loved too long.

But Jimmy was just on the other side of that window, and she could picture him smiling now as he dressed. She had been a good friend, had helped him with his act, encouraged him to be brave. Once, she'd told him she thought they were twins, psychic twins—almost identical. He'd been so moved, and they'd gone dancing together. But she had never—except for the photographs—asked anything of him. The last time they'd seen each other—a chance, brief run-in in the Waverly Street subway six months or so ago—he'd said she looked pale, tired. She told him she was depressed, but when he asked if there was anything he could do, she'd stood silent. Then her train had come, she'd smiled and kissed him goodbye.

Now Zee lifted the camera from around her neck and sat down against the building opposite Jimmy's hotel. Shivering with sweat, crying lightly and looking up at Jimmy's window, she knew she was on an irreversible course: Jimmy was probably punching out a last cigarette, and would then walk over to the window to look for her.

The White Gloves

It was almost closing time in the haberdashery. Outside, the gas lanterns were being lit throughout Chelsea—a lamplighter had just turned the corner from Redburn Street where Sophie shared a flat with Henri. She had come to find him a farewell gift and was considering a pair of white gloves; the fingers fluttered now as she tried one on for size. Extending her own gloved hand out in front of her, she pictured the gloves sliding over Henri's strong hands. *These could never be stained or dirtied,* she thought. Then she laughed at the absurdity of her logic: as if Henri's wearing the white gloves would insure his safety in battle! But she knew if she really thought about it, even for a minute, she could just as easily cry. Because she felt the tears coming, welling up, she pressed the gloves to her lips.

"Help you, Madam Brzeska?" They had met before. It was the horribly thin clerk, made shapeless by the water in her eyes; he was sliding toward her down the long, liquid line of the glass case. "We needn't apply the merchandise to our person, please."

Sophie crossed her eyes and stuck out her tongue. Her body felt stiff from the day's work; she knew that her hair was disheveled.

"If you can't behave, Madam, you may leave." The clerk snatched the gloves out of her hands.

"Don't you touch me!" She looked around, as if for help. "Those are mine. I mean, I'll take them." She had decided beforehand that she simply could not afford to worry about the price.

"Very well then."

The clerk had just put the gloves into a wide, flat box and begun binding it with twine when Sophie felt a hand squeezing her waist. "I saw you through the window."

"Mr. Gaudier," the clerk nodded to Henri.

"That's Gaudier-*Brzeska*, please, sir." He always insisted on attaching their names. "And what is *Mamus* spending her hard-earned money on?" Henri asked her. "Something good for her bad *Pik*?"

"Never mind," she said, jerking away, paying the clerk and putting the box into her carpetbag.

Henri's clothes were smudged with plaster and his satchel bulged under his arm. Sophie sensed the impatient, youthful energy in his lithe body as he stood next to her, and turned to face him. "I wasn't quite ready for you." She was flustered, idly trying to replace the loose strands of hair that had fallen out of the bun at the nape of her neck. "You seem awfully happy for a boy going off to the Front tomorrow."

"I'm happy because I am once again with my *Zosienka*."

She did not believe him. She knew that he *was* happy about going off to war, but she had resolved—since this was their last night, and because the previous days had been so awful between them—to get along and not to make any scenes.

The bell on the shop door rang as it closed behind them.

"That ghastly man probably thinks I really am your mother!"

Henri laughed. "So what? So you have twenty years more than me." Then he leaned down and whispered: "Only in love are you my *Mamuska*."

Outside, the air was cool and the September sky swatched with purple and orange. *Violently beautiful*, Henri had once described this particular type of sunset—words Sophie would never have thought to combine. All the lanterns were lit now, and the flames, with the wind, licked at the sides of the glass, leaving a black tongue print.

Until two weeks ago, Sophie had been working as a governess in Littlehampton, when Henri convinced her they should live together again, especially now that he had a studio. And so she'd given up her position and come to London. But she was immediately horrified by the living conditions Henri expected her to share, and they had fought bitterly. No sooner had they recovered from that than England and France declared war on Germany, and Henri enlisted.

"Why," Sophie had asked him, "after refusing to serve the first time you were called, do you *rush* to serve now? I don't understand it."

"Why?" Henri had raised his voice. "You know why. They told me I'd never return to France if I didn't."

"So what? You hate the French." Sophie was flushed.

"Yes, but there are Mother and Father, and especially my precious little sister, Renée."

"They are more important, I suppose. . . ."

And this went on; they had quarreled horribly.

Two nights earlier Henri was supposed to have left, did leave in fact—with both he and Sophie still furious and not speaking to one another. Because now they had a second chance, a fortunate coincidence having nothing to do with their desire to set things right but with the logistics of the French Army, they had resolved to be sweet to one another for this last night together; this gift.

"Mamuska!" When Henri walked into the room he could see that Sophie must have worked all day—just to make the place nice—while he was at the studio. She had cleaned, tidied, packed his clothes, shopped for food, and she had decorated the slab, stone walls with his sketches and studies for his sculpture: nude men and women, heads, faun, dancers, wild animals at the zoo in motion. Looking at his sketches on the walls now, Henri knew they were not perfect in form, but they had *life, energy*—and *that* was what he was after. He especially liked how he had captured the tiger's gait.

"Oh, *Zosik*." Henri picked her up and whirled her around. There was a smile pushing out the corners of her mouth—he could see it—but she got control of herself. When he put her down, she smoothed out her dress.

"I'm happy you like it."

"Yes," he nodded. "And you like my work," he gestured toward the walls. "But, *Zosienka*. Do you," he asked, taking a sketchbook out of his satchel and opening it to a drawing of a male nude, "do you like *this*?" He pointed to the genitals. "You'd better," he laughed, "for it's your very own *Pipik*."

Sophie reddened, then laughed, too.

Relieved, Henri looked around to take in the rest of the room, and he immediately noticed that the windowless flat was light for the first time! Sophie had set out so many candles; logs glowed in the fireplace. And she had rearranged the furniture. In the far corner against the wall, she had decorated her bed—a large, lumpy envelope of fabric stuffed with rags and covered with a quilt—with scarves and a silvery shawl. Opposite her oversized bed was his hard, narrow cot; and on the other side of the room, her writing desk sat positioned between the chiffonier and the door to the water closet, behind which was another very small room, furnished with only a tub.

Henri focused on the small, purple-cloth-covered table that Sophie had placed between their beds. On top was a bottle of red wine, two glasses, two tin plates, a loaf of bread, and sausage.

"Bless you, *Zosik*. I am starved."

Sophie pulled a box of sweetcakes tied with a red ribbon from her bag and sat it on the floor beside the table, then plopped down in one of the chairs. Henri could feel that she was tired and nervous. "You're afraid, aren't you—of the war?"

She nodded. She said she despised the Germans, and that she felt the darkness of the war closing in on her. But Henri knew she was also afraid she would spoil everything tonight, all her effort; afraid they would quarrel. She was always worrying.

It appeared now that she didn't quite know what to do with herself. She stood up and handed him a flat box, a gift, she said, with one hand supporting it from underneath and the other hand on its lid.

How disembodied and almost abstract Sophie's hand looked flat against the box top! He enveloped her hands with his as he took the box from her. "*Merci.* Shall I try to guess what it is?"

"No! Just unwrap it."

The rough twine scratched at his fingers as he tore the binding off the package. He could feel Sophie watching him intently; he opened the box and lifted off the lid. "They're beautiful, *Zosik.*"

"Put them on."

He took the gloves out of the box and slid them over his hands.

"They fit," Sophie said, pleased.

"Yes, they do!" Henri flashed his hands at her, palms out. "And now I feel the urge to work. They are so smooth, they'll be perfect for casting." He gave her a quick kiss on the cheek: "Off to the studio!"

She looked horrified. "Henri, no!"

In his excitement and quick movements, he stepped on the box of sweetcakes, crushing it.

"Henri!" Sophie screamed. "You . . . you *cow!*"

Henri winked, took the gloves off, brought one to his mouth, and blew; it quickly filled with his breath. Then he turned the inflated glove upside down, pulled at the plump fingers, and lowed: "Moo-oo. Mooo-ooooo."

Sophie giggled, and Henri grabbed her hands and they twirled around the floor in a dance, stopping suddenly.

"Oh! I almost forgot," he said, pulling several items from his satchel and handing them to her. There was a large sheaf of powder blue paper, a pen, and a bottle of ink. "I want you to finish your novel while I'm gone so I can read it when I come back."

"Yes, I will, Henri. I will do it; that will be my life's blood while you are away."

He watched as she put the paper to her nose and sniffed, then rubbed it against the side of her face.

"I will finish the novel and together we will greet you at the door. You will be back, won't you, *Pik*?"

"Of course I will be back. And soon thereafter, *Zosik* and her novel will be the toast of London; and *Pik* will have a show at the Leicester Galleries, and oh, but I am famished, *Zosienka*. Let's eat!"

He sat down at the table and began pouring wine into their glasses; Sophie sat across from him. "But first a toast: to *Zosik* and her *Pipik*." Sophie smiled, raised her glass and met Henri's midair.

After a gulp of wine, he asked, "Did you work on it today?"

She reddened. "Well, no, I had no time, you see, I was busy getting ready for tonight, trying to make things look nice, shopping."

"But what's more important, *Zosik*?"

"Well," she looked around the room, gesturing with her hands. "But don't you like what I've done?"

"Yes, of course, but—" But Henri realized it was best left unsaid. This was one of their old arguments: he often felt that Sophie was too dependent on comfort, too bourgeois, to be a great artist. And when he told her so, they fought about it—as they had many times.

Now, they were both painfully quiet, avoiding looking at each other—tearing off chunks of bread, slicing the sausage with a penknife, drinking.

Sophie was hurt and wanted to think of something nice, so she said, "We will just miss celebrating your twenty-third birthday, so let us celebrate it tonight!"

Henri remained silent. He remembered that it had been close to the occasion of his nineteenth birthday when they had first met. It was in the St. Genevieve Library in Paris.

Sophie had gone nightly to learn German, and with the hope of meeting someone nice. And he had been at the library studying anatomy from books and doing quick sketches of the people around him, including her.

She had told him that she was aware of him immediately, of what she called his feline features and panther-like energy. She knew he sometimes sketched her, and she was flattered. Henri was attracted to her and later told her he thought she had a tough sensuality. They had noticed each other over many successive evenings, when he finally waited for her on the front steps at closing time. He introduced himself, and then they walked to her hotel in the Rue Cajas, talking all the while. Parting that night, they agreed to meet the next day at the Louvre.

"Remember what you said about Rodin our first day together?" Sophie asked him. Rodin was Henri's favorite sculptor, a subject she knew he was always eager to discuss.

Henri smiled. "Yes. We had just seen Rodin's 'Old Woman,' which you thought ugly; and I told you it was only age, and that age shows character and is beautiful—like my *Zosik*. Because beauty is life and life has three phases: birth, maturity, and death, all of which are beautiful."

"Yes!" Sophie shivered and grabbed the shawl from her bed, wrapping it around her shoulders. "You have taught me so much, *Pik*, and you teach me still, every day."

Henri softened looking at Sophie's face. "Ah, but *Zosik*. You, too, have given me so much. I couldn't have made it through these hard times without you. We talked about art, and I came to understand my own thoughts and feelings. And Tolstoy!—you gave me Tolstoy: so much about the Slavs—whom I now love. And I will always remember what you said to me that first night, after our long day together."

Sophie looked puzzled.

"I had been telling you how lonely I was, remember? and how much I wanted someone to understand me. Oh, I re-member it so well: we were sitting in your room at the hotel, it was very late—and you told me you no longer believed in love, that after all your experiences you found life cruel and ugly. But then—and this is when I saw your true spirit—right after that you turned to me and you said: 'I am too old for you, really, but I will be a mother for you.'"

He took her hand and pressed it to his lips. "And so you have."

"And you, at such a young age, Henri, such a tender child, you have made life bearable for me; you have helped me to have a little faith, and you have improved my outlook. . . ."

As Sophie continued, Henri could no longer hear her, for he was thinking about this very tendency of hers—when excited—to go on a bit too much. It was what had ruined his friendship with Murry and Katherine Mansfield, what kept Sophie and him so isolated and without friends—sometimes he felt he would go mad with it! She couldn't understand his need for other people; she was always saying it meant that he didn't love her enough.

He looked at her—she was still talking—and remembered how unfairly Katherine had treated Sophie, and how he had defended her. But he wanted things to change when he came back, and he believed they could change. He looked up now to see her face shining on him.

"What is it, Henri?"

He shook his head. "Nothing."

She yawned. "I am so tired, Henri. I want us to be awake all night, to make the most of our last moments together. But you must be rested for tomorrow."

"Yes, but I could stay up all night, *Zosik*."

Sophie ignored him and went around the room blowing out the candles except for the one by her bed.

"All right," he said. "I will try to sleep if you will sing to me the song about the woman who has jumped into the well to drown herself."

It was an old Polish folk song she had sung to him once on holiday.

"Oh, *Pik*, I'm so tired," she said. But he could see she was pleased at his request. "Let's move the table back against the wall, and get ready for bed. Then I will sing."

She put the remains of their dinner on the mantel, and together they moved the table and chairs up against the wall next to her desk. She took off her dress and folded it over the desk chair, then sat down on her bed wearing the tattered, pink silk chemise she had bought in Paris before her savings had dwindled, before Henri. Finally, she began to sing.

Henri watched the shadow of her head move on the wall in the candlelight as she gestured; her voice was sweet and plaintive. Sophie had always *become* the part when she sang; now she was that lost girl. Tears ran down her cheeks as she finished the song.

Henri caught a glimpse of her fine, delicate profile as she turned to blow out the last candle, and he remembered running his hands over the surface of her face with his eyes closed in preparation for the bust he would do of her.

She turned back to him now, and he thanked her for the song, then kissed her on the forehead. That bust was gone now, he thought sadly; he had destroyed it in one of their fights.

"I wish you peace," Sophie said, cupping her hand on the side of his face.

In the darkness, Henri pulled his cot up next to hers so that they might hold hands on their last night together.

Her hand slackened within minutes, and then her irregular, ragged snoring began. Henri looked at her in the darkness but could see only the outline of her body shrouded under the quilt. And like so many times before, he wanted her, wanted to express his love for her completely, physically. But he knew Sophie wouldn't have it; he had tried. And he *understood* how she felt, he knew that it was *because* she loved him that she wouldn't allow it; she had even let him have other women, men, too, when he felt the need. But still, he was often "overcome by sex feelings," as he put it to her, frustrated. He closed his eyes to try to focus on something else. He thought of all Sophie had done for him, of how she had saved him from loneliness, from himself, really, and the indulgences of youth. She had comforted him, nursed him, had always made their quarters nice, and she had used up all of her savings, had bought his supplies again and again—over the years. But mostly, she had listened to him, talked with him, about art. Soon he would be gone, and all their problems would fade; it would be only their spirits communing in letters. He knew he would miss her; at times he even wondered if he could survive without her. Still, he was looking forward to experiencing war; it would give him the opportunity to see a whole new kind of movement he had never seen before. He had been to wrestling and boxing matches, and had sketched from them, but this would be different; the *motivation* would be different. Wrestling and boxing were merely sports, whereas war—war was serious. Rodin had said that the only important thing in sculpture was to express life, and Henri felt sure he would see the life both in and out of the body in a new way, and that it would change his work when he came back.

He thought all night, didn't sleep, and got up with the first light, stoked the fire, lay in a few more logs, then boiled water for tea on Sophie's small, porcelain oil stove. He ate what was left of the sausage from the night before, drank his tea, and on a sheet of the blue paper he had bought her, he sketched Sophie sleeping.

Sophie woke up with the six o'clock bells from the near-by church and made tea for herself and Henri. They drank in silence, looking at each other, knowing they had less than one hour together; at seven Henri was due to meet a small regiment down at the mouth of the Thames. Sophie's eyes teared up at the thought of him leaving, of their not seeing one another for so long, and she berated herself for all the wrong she had done him, all her recriminations. She wouldn't blame him if he decided to remain in France with his parents and Renée after the war and never come back. She had always loved him more, *needed* him more.

But when the time came for Henri to leave, his eyes, too, surprisingly, were full of tears.

"I love you, *Zosik*," he said, embracing her. (Now, he felt frightened for the first time). "I will love you all the while I am gone, and still—when I return. Always."

Sophie couldn't speak, but nodded and sobbed. Henri put on his beret, picked up his satchel and another bag, then opened the door. Sophie followed him out, wearing only her chemise.

Embracing her one last time, Henri said, "Goodbye, *Zosik*."

Sophie tried to control herself, wanting Henri to remember a smooth, pleasant face. She ran out into the street and waved for as long as they could see each other, until Henri had turned onto Flood Street and the buildings were between them. And then he was gone. She ran back into the flat, slammed the door behind her, and sat down on the floor with her head on Henri's hard cot, sobbing: *He is gone. He is gone. He is gone. . . .*

Oh, how she had suffered! That half-moon in her family crest had brought her such bad luck throughout her life. Her father had treated her and her mother so badly, always wishing aloud, this man with four sons, that his only daughter had not been born; keeping mistresses and spending his money on them to such an extent that kept the family poor. Yes, she had suffered. She had blindly followed lovers and jobs to Cracow, Paris, New York, Philadelphia, London; the lovers always made promises they did not keep. They got what they wanted from her, used her up, and then left her. That was why she would not allow anything between herself and Henri, because she didn't believe it; her eyes were wide open now, her vision clear, and she saw that love and sex simply should not be combined. If Henri didn't exactly understand—and how could he, he was so young—at least he respected her wishes. Yes, she had suffered, and here she was now suffering again. But this was different. Now she was taken seriously, treated fairly, living fully in the world. She had her novel. And look!—there at the end of it all, she was loved. She could say that—she had been loved, for she knew Henri loved her.

When she fell back to sleep, Sophie felt warm and enveloped in a soft cocoon; protected.

Within weeks after Henri left England, Sophie took another governess position, this one in nearby Kensington so she could commute and keep their flat in Chelsea. She thought Henri would be proud of her, and he was.

"But all I can give you from here," he wrote, "is a buttercup; the only flower that grows in the trenches."

Henri wrote to her frequently. "I implore my *Zosik* to work hard and regularly on her novel, at least five hours a day."

Sophie wrote back less frequently. She wasn't working on the novel, there were too many distractions and interruptions; she wasn't a machine. She told Henri that she missed him terribly, and that she was feeling very alone.

While Henri never flinched from depicting the war and the difficulties of life at the front, his letters were always full of youthful energy and expressions of undying love for his *Zosik*; often he enclosed little sketches he had done. He only wished Sophie would write him more often; he said he needed her.

When Sophie lost her job, her employer told her she had a "difficult personality," she put off writing to Henri. Finally she told him, and went on to say that she was unhappy, hated England, and that it was all his fault; after all, he had brought her there. After posting that letter she quickly wrote another, to apologize.

But just one day after her forty-third birthday, on June 7, Sophie received a telegram from Capitaine B. Menager, commander of the 129th infantry. He wrote that Henri had been killed in action on June 5 at Neuville St. Vaast, at approximately one in the afternoon. Sophie fainted.

Later, in a note received along with Henri's belongings, Capitaine Menager wrote that Sophie would be proud to know Henri had served his country well and had recently been promoted to Sergeant. The Capitaine also said he thought it might interest her to see that Henri had done small bits of sculpture from the butts of rifles using his penknife while in the trenches, and that these were enclosed. "He loved the walnut wood that the German rifles are made from," the Capitaine wrote.

But Sophie was not comforted. She was in a fury. Because among Henri's possessions, she could not find the gloves she had given him. She tore through the contents of the brown, paper-wrapped package again and again, to no avail. *The Capitaine probably kept them for himself,* she thought. *I must have them.*

She goes through the package one last time, with no luck. But then, suddenly, she sees the gloves, just as they were on her last night with Henri—when they were briefly infused with his breath, before shriveling. They are lying on a field in Neuville St. Vaast, unstained and inflated, like white birds—*because Henri would fly away.* She watches the gloves now as they leave the ground, ascend, and thinks: *they have his life.*

Relieved Occasionally
by a Primary Color

"I *could* stop at the library and pick up a Mondrian book for you." Patsy is ready to go out the door. She is wearing jeans, a man's oversized dress shirt (not necessarily Jack's) and her old, black raincoat—something she rarely leaves home without. Patsy is what Jack's mother refers to as "a big girl," meaning not fat but tall and big-boned.

Jack looms in the kitchen doorway, glasses low on his nose, and whispers, "No. I don't want to know."

"You're lazy, Jack," Patsy says. She gives her long graying-brown hair a final brushing.

"Hey, give me a break, will you. Life is tough enough as it is." He walks over to her, smiling, then cups his hand along the side of her face. "Really, it isn't laziness, Pats. It's that I don't want to know; I don't want this to be happening. Not this week, anyway. I've got to keep my focus on the show."

They had been fighting earlier that morning, over nothing really, it was just tension; *Jack's* tension: he is frenetically preparing for an exhibit. "You're driving me to abstraction!" Patsy finally said, cracking them up.

It wasn't easy, two artists, good-sized people at that, living together for almost twenty years now in the same small studio in New York City; but that they genuinely liked each other helped.

Patsy is heading out on one of her infamous scavenging trips, hoping to turn up some things she can use in her work. Like her hero and mentor Joseph Cornell, she assembles boxes, only hers are not diminutive but extra large, usually with a bit of Dali's influence thrown in, so that they often resemble the oversized, severed rooms of a warped doll-house. Her purpose, Patsy has always said, is to point out the absurdity and otherness of *things*, and to have fun. These forays are still exciting to her, and on a good day she might turn up an alarm clock, a manual eggbeater, a "Slinky," a hair dryer, a deflated beach ball, a waffle iron. . . .

"America!" she always says coming back after a good hunt, "land of plenty!"

Unlike Jack, Patsy has stuck with more or less the same style over a twenty-year period.

Over his twenty-five year career, Jack has tried on a series of styles and can only wonder why now, when he is finally painting big and free, more freely than ever—the very approach he has so long been striving toward and which seems most organic and natural—can only wonder why the image which comes to him now every time he approaches the canvas, which returns again and again, relentlessly, is this: the Dutch painter Piet Mondrian walking to post a letter in Paris: *The streets are slicked black with rain, the sky is a deep blue, the streetlights glow yellow, and the postbox shines Chinese red. His movements crisp and precise, Mondrian walks (carrying the letter, a small white rectangle, at his side) as if magnetized from beneath the sidewalk, and then turns, sharp, on the right angle.*

Jack tells Patsy that his vision of the scene is from overhead, so that Mondrian's path looks like a map ("the map of a rather anal cartographer, mind you") and that Mondrian is represented by the small, black circle of his bowler hat.

"It's like seeing the same scene of a film over and over," he explains to her, "as if you were on the set witnessing the director, unsatisfied, ordering take after take after take. "'Take 57!'" Jack cups his hands to simulate a megaphone. "'Mondrian walks down a Paris street to mail a letter. *Action!*'"

Patsy sits on a stool at the kitchen counter, eating toast and drinking coffee. "You've been under a lot of pressure," she begins, her old line.

"Okay, so maybe I have." Jack throws up his hands. "But why Mondrian—of all people! He's a professional control freak: the primary colors, the grid systems, all that geometry!"

"But how do you know it's Mondrian if all you can see is his hat?"

He looks at her. "I just know."

"Well, maybe he has something to say to you."

Jack glares at her over the rim of his coffee mug.

"I'm serious. You remember that time I heard Joseph Cornell's voice coming from one of his works at the Met? Maybe the letter Mondrian's mailing is for you."

"Yeah, and maybe he's really Mephistopheles."

Patsy laughs, and Jack, at least, almost cracks a smile. "I mean it's the complete opposite of what I'm doing now."

"I could put Mondrian in one of my boxes for you," she says wryly, "and put the lid on."

After Patsy has left to go scavenging, Jack stands once again before an empty canvas. He is glad she's gone; he needs to be alone right now. He steps back from the blank, white monster. This Mondrian image has been recurring to him for over two weeks, and he is determined to beat it. His show is now only five days away, and he has one painting left to finish. He walks over to the tall, floor-to-ceiling windows that look out over the street, picks up another canvas leaning against the wall, this one much smaller and square, approximately four by four, and rests it against the larger one. Then he quickly draws what he sees in his mind (*"I'll get it out of my system," he tells himself*). He draws the black bands of Paris streets, paints the indigo wash of sky, splotches a yellow streetlight, and cubes a red postbox. For Mondrian himself, or rather for his bowler hat, he dips a perfect, unbent beer bottle cap in black paint and presses it against the canvas—somewhere over the line, approximating 3-D head level—and then releases it.

"There," he says. Enjoying himself, he leans back, hand on his hip; but then he is immediately seized with the realization that by painting his vision, he has also painted something *like* a Mondrian.

He walks into the kitchen, grabs a beer from the fridge, and pads back into the studio, throwing himself down on the sofa he and Patsy positioned in the middle of the room. He doesn't know much about Mondrian, other than what he's seen, mostly at the Museum of Modern Art. And yet, later that afternoon, after a couple more beers, he finds himself sitting down and reading about him. Both Jack and Patsy try to avoid reading theory as much as possible, preferring that their approach be intuitive rather than intellectual, but Patsy does own two art history books, Janson's *History of Art*, and the volume he now reads from, Fleming's *Arts and Ideas*:

"His colors are likewise abstract—black lines of various widths against white backgrounds, relieved occasionally by a primary color "climax"—red, blue, or yellow—in as pure a state as possible. . . . In his early years, Mondrian painted landscapes and quiet interior scenes in the tradition of his native Holland, and his later style, though completely abstract, owes much to the cool geometrical precision of his great predecessor Vermeer."

"Vermeer!" Never in a million years would he have come up with that! What was this crap? Jack picks up the book again and looks at the representations of Mondrian's paintings, then at a few Vermeers. And there it is: the blues and golds, the black-and-white chessboard floors: geometry. He remembers how, as an undergraduate, he had lain in bed for the longest time looking at a print of Vermeer's "The Letter" on the opposite wall; he had crossed his eyes so as to blur representation and see only the forms, the shapes of the painting—how orderly and pleasing they were. Yes, it was true: Mondrian from Vermeer.

He gets up from the sofa, grabs a note-pad, and writes to Patsy: "Going to MOMA to see you-know-who. Home by six. Love, J-man."

When Mondrian greets him inside the Museum of Modern Art, Jack is not surprised; he recognizes him immediately. Wearing a black suit and holding the bowler hat in his long, slender, knotty hands, he looks exactly as he did in photographs: small, balding, with a fine nose, feral eyes and round wire-rim glasses. Neither speaks as the painter takes Jack's elbow and leads him through a maze of rooms, walking past Picasso's "Les Demoiselles D'Avignon" as if it were a fire hydrant, and then breezing through

Monet's crowded, sunny "Waterlilies" room; and on, passing partitions, until—suddenly—they are standing before Mondrian's "Composition in White, Black, and Red."

"Look!" Mondrian says, his eyes gleaming with water and light.

Jack stands looking at the painting for a while, the Dutchman at his side, and he sees something beyond geometry: the lifetime of thought and inspiration behind Mondrian's work. Then, because it seems the only appropriate thing to do, he bows from the waist to the dead painter.

When Jack walks in the door of the studio, Patsy immediately hugs him and regales him with her finds: a curling iron, several strands of silver and green garland, a blender. "A moderate success," she says. "Oh, and the mail—I got a letter from Mimi."

"Mondrian was waiting for me at MOMA today."

"Yeah, sure," she says. "And I found several pieces of the Duchess of Windsor's jewelry in somebody's trash."

"Patsy, I'm serious!"

"Okay, Jack. Okay. So tell me what happened."

"Well, not much, really. He just led me to his paintings and told me to look."

"And?"

"And I did."

"Want to talk about it some more over Chinese?"

Jack doesn't answer her; he is lost picturing Mondrian back at the museum.

"Chinese, Jack? I'm hungry."

"Oh," he says, snapping to, "sure."

Patsy puts on the raincoat, Jack grabs his Army jacket, and they go out the door. At the top of the landing, as Patsy locks the double lock, Jack stands looking down the steep flight of stairs. He says, "You know, if I took off all my clothes right now I'd be 'Nude Descending a Staircase.'"

Patsy pushes back her hair, then grins and frowns in rapid succession. "Yeah, and if I shoved you down the stairs you'd be mashed potatoes."

Talking constantly, they walk through the twilit streets to their favorite restaurant in Chinatown. The small, red room is almost empty—one man sits eating alone, reading, and another couple is talking animatedly and slopping up Dun Dun Noodle. Patsy and Jack get their favorite table, in the front by the window, and once seated they order and are immediately served, two beers.

"You know, I think you're taking all of this too seriously, Jack, you're missing the fun."

"But he really was there, Pats!"

"I don't mean about Mondrian—I believe you. I mean your work."

"That's easy for you to say. You don't have a show in five days."

The waiter comes and takes their order. After he leaves, they drink for a moment in silence.

"Don't get mad, Jack" she says finally, looking at him through the golden neck of her beer bottle. "I just hate to see you so tortured. I mean the critics are going to say what they want, and *at least* fifty percent of the time it's going to be negative. But so what? It doesn't have anything to do with why you paint."

Jack sits up as the waiter brings their Suan La Chow Show. "Can we just eat this in peace?" he asks.

Hurt, she nods.

But he feels immediately guilty. "So, you got a letter from little sister? How is she?"

Patsy brightens, chewing on a spicy won ton. "Mimi's good. She told me the most amazing story. Ooh, this is hot." She is sniffling.

"Just the way we like it, huh, honey?" he says, aping blissful coupledom. "What did she say?"

"Well, you know Mimi's had a new job for a couple of months now, working for this agency taking care of old people."

"Yeah."

"And so far all of her clients have been rich, and. . . ." She stops and watches as the waiter sets down the rest of their dinner. She begins dishing up her plate, "Anyway, she's been taking care of this seventy-six-year-old woman with Alzheimer's for the past month or so. The woman, Caroline, was an artist; her husband was too. Mimi says some of his stuff is hanging in the Museum of Fine Arts there in Boston."

She stops to take a long swig of her beer, then removes the letter from her raincoat pocket, lifts it out of the envelope, unfolds it, and reads: "*Caroline is obsessed with the Museum of Fine Arts, and wants to go all the time.*" And so the people who work with her, like Mimi, take her. Mimi says Caroline goes there probably four times a week, and whenever she can't go, like on Mondays when the museum's closed, she gets in a really bad mood. And yet, Mimi says sometimes when she and Caroline are leaving the Museum, walking to the car Caroline will say, 'When are we going to Fine Arts?'"

"God, it must be so frustrating."

"Yeah, but I haven't even told you the really amazing part yet." She looks down at the letter again, then back up at him. "First off, Mimi says she's got some really great paintings in her apartment: a Rothko, a de Kooning—stuff like that. She lives in a high-rise overlooking the Charles."

Jack's eyes widen. "*Must* be rich."

"And she says Caroline's work is hanging all over the place, too, and that it's really good. So Mimi's taken her to the M.F.A. probably at least ten times in the past month, right? She'll show Caroline the Impressionist stuff, and Caroline will say, 'I don't much care for that.' But no matter where they are in the museum, Caroline can always find the Pollocks. Mimi says she herself gets confused, but Caroline always knows. Order us a couple of more beers, will you?"

Jack raises two fingers to get the waiter's attention and asks for two more beers, which are delivered within seconds.

"Anyway," she takes a small sip, "Mimi says Caroline really glows when she sees the Pollocks." Patsy looks down at the letter again. "And here, listen to this: Mimi says it's not just a fluke either, because you can see Pollock's influence in Caroline's own work."

Patsy folds the letter, puts it back in its envelope and into her coat pocket. "Oh, and she says to tell you she'll be down Saturday for your show."

"Oh yeah, my show." His face dims. "I'd almost forgotten." Jack turns quiet, tucks back into himself again.

"Sulking?" Patsy asks, reaching across the table and shaking him. "Don't you get anything from that story?"

"Yeah," Jack answers, "I guess so."

"And so?"

"So what?"

"Well," she says, taking his arm, "where does that take you with your own work, with the show?"

He looks at her. "I guess what gets me is how Pollock's effect on this woman, his energy maybe, can even push through her disease." He pauses, peels away at the label of his beer bottle, then looks back up at Patsy. "You know, this afternoon I read about Mondrian in one of your art history books."

"And what happened?"

"Well, it made me feel bad. I just started wondering what the meaning of my work is, where it comes from: things like that."

She opens her mouth to say something, but he puts a finger over her lips and continues.

"But I know you'd say to me—look: here's this woman who can't know anything about meaning anymore, but she responds, she finds some relief."

"Exactly!" Patsy exclaims.

"Relief," Jack says ponderously. "Relief. Relief." Suddenly, he snaps his fingers. "'Relieved occasionally by a primary color.'"

"What?" Patsy is confused. "You've lost me."

"It's what I read this afternoon, about Mondrian."

They are silent as the waiter brings the check. Patsy fishes for the cash in her raincoat pocket. "What a wonderful phrase, Jack, don't you think? I mean, it's what art is."

"Is and does," Jack adds, smiling, as they leave the restaurant.

Walking out into the carnival of Chinatown at night, Jack notices that it has begun to rain; the red and yellow neon lights bloom on the slick black pavement.

"All it needs is a little blue," he says, pointing to the painting of lights on the street and taking Patsy's arm.

Patsy rolls her eyes. "You and Mondrian!"

Billy's Blues

This Close
July 1987

Billy had worked in the neighborhood liquor store for years, a slight man in his late thirties with dark hair and hurt, fearful eyes; I used to see him most every Thursday afternoon walking down Elm Street with his mother, his arms filled with bags of groceries. She was a pale, vulnerable-looking woman, with jet black hair and eyebrows the shape of McDonald's arches, who sailed toward the square full-steam, seeming to pull Billy along in her current. I wasn't surprised to learn much later that he still lived with her.

It was his eyes that pulled you in: brown, slightly turned-down at the ends, as if he were tucking them in for protection, the way a turtle goes into its shell. You wanted to hold him. Or at least I did.

I used to go into the liquor store just to see him. Once, a chubby co-worker, his older brother Jack I later found out, yelled, "Billy, get your butt out here!" and Billy walked out of the stockroom, smiling—which is how I knew his name years before I actually knew him. I would always buy something, a beer or a bottle of wine, to justify my presence.

Rarely, very rarely, Billy would be at the register, and when he was, I might as well have been standing there naked: the eyes acknowledging, hands touching—exchanging money, lips parting for a smile, or to say—what? Thanks. Have a nice night. Do you want a bag? Do you want to sleep with me? That was what I wanted to hear.

I had been working for the "Somerville Journal"—their first "girl reporter"—for eight years and had been through plenty of men, just not the men I wanted; none like Billy. And for the first three years that I lived in the neighborhood and saw Billy working in the store, I was living with some-one. Whenever things weren't going well between us I'd fantasize asking Billy to have coffee with me, which is what happened, eventually.

It was a couple of months after Bob moved out, a hot Saturday when I'd grown tired of sitting around analyzing what had gone wrong. Impulsively, I walked the ten-minute walk to the liquor store and saw Billy putting bottles of "Cossack" vodka on the shelf. I asked him if he got a break, and he said that he did, so I asked if he would have coffee with me. He smiled, said he would, and then told his brother he wouldn't be long.

We didn't talk much that first day, mostly sat and looked at each other over sips of coffee. I did tell him I had been thinking about him and about doing what we were doing then for years, and he surprised me by saying that he knew, then asked if he could come over to my place that night.

So began what was to become an almost nightly occur-rence for the next four months. Billy came that night after eleven when the store closed. I had showered, put on my favorite kimono, and turned the lights down low. I asked him if he'd like a glass of wine, and he said he didn't drink, that his brother Jack did the drinking in the family, but that he *would* like to take a shower, if it was all right.

We spent the rest of the night in bed, and that—with increasing conversation—was how our nights went. We never left my apartment together.

Billy told me he lived with his mother, and that the liquor store was a family business his father had started back in the late Fifties. His brother Jack took over when their father died in '75, Billy said, but Jack wasn't the favorite. When their father was dying, he'd taken Billy aside: "'You were always my best son,' he told me, 'you look after your mother for me. You're the only one that can.'" Billy promised he would. It was a frustrating life, he said, but his mother needed him, in her way. He said sometimes he felt so trapped that he would dream of jumping a boxcar to nowhere in particular, anywhere.

Billy had been with only a few women over the years, casually, and said that—except for a male friend he once had—what he had with me was the closest to what you could call a relationship. He said going into me was like going into the world.

For me, sex with Billy was something new, not casual; he was so intense, so contained and frustrated. I felt as though an arrow had come from way out in the universe, into me.

Toward the end he told me his mother didn't like his staying out so often, and that we might have to stop; or, that he would have to go home some nights. I wondered if this was true, or if he was just beginning to pull away.

The night he didn't come I didn't know what to think. He had told me never to call him at home, so I tried his work number (even though it was after midnight). But there was no answer, so I got dressed and walked down to the liquor store.

Billy's death was as senseless as many things are in this life: the guy told the police he was having D.T.'s and didn't mean to kill anybody, that he just needed the booze; the senselessness compounded by the fact that it could just as easily *not* have happened; a slight change in time, or response, and Billy would still be alive.

Recently I saw Billy's mother on the street, but only from the back; I recognized her by the sad way her black raincoat was hunched up at the neck—just as it had at Billy's funeral.

Yes, I went, though I thought the idea of Billy being buried was absurd, redundant even: Billy's life was like a box, a box he leaves me holding that, when the four sides, top and bottom are ripped off, opens onto emptiness, emptiness and a wide longing.

Five O'clock Shadow
January 1979

You're not supposed to still be living with your mother at your age, time's passing, but what can you do? You tried to leave but you just couldn't do it. Your father told you right before he died five years ago to take care of your mother; you promised, and you try, you really try, but jesus, you feel so boxed in. You work fifty-some hours a week, at the liquor store that your older brother Jack took over. It's never regular and you don't bring home all that much since it's a family business. Jack's an alkie who doesn't give much of a damn about anything, especially you, or her (*his* mother, too, you want to remind him) or even his own wife and three kids; all he seems to care about is where his next drink is coming from.

She gets a little money from the government, but you're responsible for just about everything else. You run her errands and go to the market with her every Thursday—on foot because she won't let you buy a car, she's afraid you'll be in an accident—and then you sit at home with her and watch TV those nights you don't work, which is only two or three a week. You sleep late into the day because only in sleep is your time your own, only there are you released, and so you sleep, sometimes until one or even two in the afternoon, when you have to go in at three.

You're only thirty-one but people say you look older. "You're so pale, Billy," they say. "And those dark circles

under your eyes. You're ruining your health." This is people
who come into the store, and relatives; you really don't have
any friends. But at least you don't drink, you want to say,
not a drop, but you can't say it since it's a liquor store, it
wouldn't be good business. Sometimes, not often enough,
you actually do something else, like on Sunday when the
store's closed; after taking her to church you go to a movie
or just hang out in the park and smell the honeysuckle. You
like the sweet smell because it reminds you of the freedom
of those seventy-eight days when you'd moved out and lived
on your own.

There was a honeysuckle bush winding around the
peeling, white banister on the porch of the house you moved
into. It was spring going into summer then and stayed light
until eight-thirty or nine, god there was so much light! But
now, you sit in the park and it gets dark so early and you
watch other people and wonder what their lives are like and
how they get through. They have children, husbands, wives,
lovers; they laugh a lot. You're not sure you believe it all,
but you think about running away anyway.

You wake up most afternoons into a dark room with the
mid-day sun cutting through dusty Venetian blinds. You
drink coffee, talk to her. Sometimes she tries to run things
like some Marine drill sergeant or something, which she got
from him. She irons your clothes and her own until everything's stiff and creased; her dyed, jet-black hair is piled
high no matter what time you get up, and her face all
made-up; meals are at the same time every day. But then
other times she just can't manage it, and she sits in the
kitchen, drinking and chain-smoking.

You're living in the same house you were brought to day
one; the same yellowing walls, the same stains everywhere,
the same furniture, the same appliances and stupid
knickknacks, the same olive and lime green fake-leaf lazy

Susan filled with her pills on the dining room table and his picture up on the mantel with never-touched-by-a-match gold candles on each side like some goddamn altar or something: everything the same, always, and you're sick to death of it. The nights you work you don't get home till 11:30 or so and then it takes you awhile to unwind. Sometimes she's up and sometimes not. Maybe you watch a talk show and then go to your room and smoke in the dark. She can walk in on you anytime without knocking if she's worrying. Sometimes you read. You hear the train when it passes behind the house late at night, just as it always has, the 2:25. Or is it five minutes early and really the 2:30? Or ten minutes late and the 2:15? You've always wondered but never checked into it. Figures. But when you feel the vibration of the train coming toward you, even before you hear it really, you imagine, as you have so often and for so long, you imagine jumping on. It's going through Boston and on up into Maine somewhere, you found out, but that doesn't matter. The train shakes the earth as it passes and you wish it would shake so hard that the house crumbled to the ground, fell into a heap; you need something to shake things up. Once, for five weeks, you thought you had found that something.

There was a man, an older college student who moved into the neighborhood. You saw him often at the liquor store; he bought only beer. And he saw you. Something happened, something was there, you don't know what, some kind of recognition or something. You're not queer or anything. But anyway things started up, and for five weeks you and this man were kind of happy together. You'd been with several women but it had never worked out. They usually ended up thinking something was wrong with you that you were still living with your mother, or they wanted to marry you and raise a family and saw that you would never leave her. One of them told you you were like a beautiful, sleek, dark-furred fox; another said a weasel. It's your eyes and your wiriness, the last one said, trying to explain the comparisons of the previous two.

But with the man, Liam, who just said you were sad-happy, you weren't acting anything or playing any games or keeping anything back, like about your mother. All your cards were on the table and you felt like this was it, really it, that this was your chance, your way out. For him it just seemed like the most natural thing in the world, and that helped you a lot. He didn't look gay at all: he had curly red hair, a great laugh and smile; he liked old movies, was tall, skinny and good at basketball, his nickname was "Spider." You can't really go into it, explain it, or even understand it. It just was.

But then one night you thought she saw the two of you together. You tried to find out later, to pump her, but you never really knew for sure. You still don't know. It was your night off. You and Liam were walking along the railroad tracks, smoking. Both of you had just showered, your hair was still wet. Liam's apartment was down the line of the tracks a few blocks, on Richdale, and you were walking home. Liam tagged along, in a playful mood, thinking up songs about trains, and then singing them. There wouldn't be a train coming through for another four hours. It was dark. You weren't worrying about anything. He was singing "I've been working on the railroad" and you had even started to join in. But then you saw her.

She had never before, not ever, in your memory, sat on the back porch. But there she was. You saw the pale, lined, puffy face barely lit up in the orange glow of her cigarette, and, for a moment, it seemed like time had stopped and you forgot everything else in the world and just wondered about the pain hidden in those creases. Her eyesight isn't so good and her glasses were propped up on top of her head so that her face looked like an open map. She seemed to be looking right at you but you just can't say for sure. You motioned Liam to "Ssh!" and ran up the bank out of her line of vision, and then onto Roseland.

Of course you could have been just walking along the railroad tracks with someone, anyone, a new friend, but part of this whole mess is that you knew she'd know, you just *knew* it. So then you started imagining all kinds of things, like her telling Jack, and everybody in the neighborhood and at the liquor store finding out; you pictured her standing in the kitchen doorway saying I'm glad your father isn't here to see this and then having some kind of a breakdown or something and ending up at Central—that kind of stuff. And so you stopped it. Just like that: on a dime.

You told him when he came into the store one day looking for you, his face all upset and everything, and asking what was wrong, why hadn't he seen you? You took him out the back door and outside by the dumpster, by all the empty boxes and the scurrying rats, and you told him it was over and to never come near you again, that you didn't know him anymore. He screamed at you and kept saying why? and broke a bottle on the side of the dumpster and cut his hand, and all you did was look around hoping nobody saw the whole thing, and then walked inside.

But then there was one more time: you arranged to meet him at midnight on the side of the warehouse that faces the tracks just off Richdale, and you told him you were sorry about how you'd treated him, that you didn't want it to be over either but that was the way you had to do it because it *had* to be over even though you didn't want it to, that it didn't matter what you wanted or what he wanted, that some things were just like that and he had to grow up and face the facts. He cried and hung onto you and you even cried a little too. And that was the last time you ever saw him; he must have moved away or something.

And it's not that she's so bad, like a real mean bitch or anything; she's not. It's not that you're some kind of jerk, either, like Jack. Because sometimes you really have fun together, playing cards late at night, talking about the old times when he was still alive, or you're just out on the street with her coming back from the market, the things she'll say, like her crack that time about Mr. Fiorucci next door always smelling like dirty ketchup. Dad always said she was very delicate and you guess he was right and that it's made her an unusual person: sometimes she's so fun to be with and other times she worries herself sick and then you too, completely out of your skin! And she's so naive and innocent sometimes. She'll be sitting there putting on her eyebrows and say something like: "Billy, honey, do you think maybe Jack is drinking too much?" And then sometimes you'll just be sitting there, maybe with the TV on, or even not on, talking, or not talking, and she'll just look at you, she might even be smiling, but you'll feel all torn up inside. She's only fifty-four now, but let's face it: if you asked her she'd tell you that her life was over five years ago when he died. You'd never ask her but you just know she feels that way; everybody knows.

And that's why in the end you just can't leave. Three years ago you did it, you talked to her, you tried to explain, you talked to Jack—who was three sheets to the wind the whole time—and then you did it. This was after Liam, but too late. You found a place just two streets down and two over, on Cogswell, where you could still hear the trains. Your Aunt Sophie and Uncle Mike had lived on the same street when you were growing up and you thought she'd like that, that it would be okay. It was a small, one-bedroom in an old house you knew and the rent wasn't bad. At first when you told her she cried and cried and stopped eating and wouldn't even get out of bed, but like always—she's listened to you more than anybody since he died—she came around, sort of. She said she'd be okay as long as you'd stop in or at least call her everyday, and then she worried about your having all the things a person needs when they set up house, she even gave you fifty dollars worth of quarters she'd saved in a jar for god knows how long.

And so you moved, the first of May it was, you had the day off and you borrowed Jack's car and moved your few things over. The night smelled so good and you stayed up late cleaning, with the radio on, smelling the honeysuckle and lilac. And then the next morning, after just a couple hours of sleep, you got up real early, made coffee and sat in the kitchen in nothing but your underwear—something you could never do at home—then dressed and went to the market by yourself, came home by cab loaded down with bundles and stocked the refrigerator and cabinets. At three you had to go in to work but the day sailed past. You called her and she seemed okay, said she'd slept like a child, and you felt so happy you told her you loved her and said she'd have to come over for dinner real soon. And that night you left work, went home, took a shower, turned on the radio and looked out the window into the deep blue sky. Time passed like that. You could probably recount what happened every single day and night you were there, you felt so alive to everything. You bought a stereo second hand and then a few records—all jazz, from the 30s, 40s and 50s—music they'd played and danced to around the house when you were growing up. You stayed up even later sometimes than you used to living with her, or you didn't and woke up before the sun and went out for a walk. You ate whenever and whatever you felt like. It seemed like even your thoughts were freer: you thought about how your job working in the store couldn't last forever since Jack was only leasing, and you pictured a future when you weren't there and worked at some other, better job, and maybe had somebody. Sometimes you didn't shave for a day or two, and Jack didn't notice or care and nobody else complained like she would have, and maybe it wasn't a big deal but it was to you; you liked the freedom of it and even the way it looked.

Once, you had asked Liam what the big deal was, why you? and he just shrugged and looked at you in that direct way he had and said because you were you, why *him*? You thought about Liam sometimes, you wondered where he was and felt sad. She would never let you be sad, would always try to tease you out of it, make you laugh or smile at least. But alone you let yourself feel sad and sometimes you spent a whole night that way, looking out the window remembering or not remembering, just listening to some sad saxophone or trumpet solo and sometimes jerking off. Since Liam you'd more or less decided that it's just *the person* that comes along, never mind their sex or color or race or religion or anything. You know in your gut that that's how *everything* in life is, who-or-whatever comes along, and anybody that thinks otherwise is kidding himself. And it either takes or it doesn't. Yet you couldn't imagine being with any other man, so thought that maybe this was your chance with a woman; and one day, with the idea of a woman in mind, no one in particular, you brought home flowers and put them in a coffee can and placed them on the small kitchen table.

All that time you called her every day religiously, still took her to the market on Thursday, to church on Sunday, and you invited her over for dinner one night a week, usually Tuesday. At first she was nice, made a big fuss about your cooking and how nice you'd fixed the place up and everything, but after a while she'd start to complain, saying she didn't think she could live by herself anymore (like she'd been doing it for a long time) and didn't know who she could get to live with her.

So one morning at the store when it's just the two of you there, Jack takes you in the back where the room's so tight with all the boxes and everything and you can hardly breathe, and he blesses you out something awful; he tells you he's sick and tired of hearing her complain, and then he tells you that she fell several days ago and what the hell are you trying to prove living on your own? just who the hell do you think you are? You say why doesn't he try living with her for a change, and he says, Because *I've* got a wife and kids. And he tells you again that she fell—in the kitchen on that rug in front of the sink.

You go home that night after the store closes and you stew, you just stew. Mad at him, mad at her, mad at the goddamn world for putting you in such a position. You feel guilty as all hell and yet you don't want to do it, you don't want to go back. It's not like you have a lot of time to waste since your life is probably almost half over already anyway. So you go out for a walk, come back and make a list of pro's and con's. And you win, but then you cancel that out, think you're just being selfish. You wait for the 2:25 and think about throwing yourself down on the tracks but you know you won't. You know what you'll do, the decision is already made: you'll sleep until however late you set the alarm for and then you'll get up, put on water for coffee and— bleary-eyed—you'll call her and say you'll move back at the end of the month. She cries and says she's sorry but you tell her everything will be fine, just like *he* used to.

And so you do, you move back: it's the middle of July and everything is the same again. Meals at set times, washing and shaving every day, going to the market on Thursday, church on Sunday, and work, work, work.

You still imagine just up and leaving, disappearing one day, jumping a boxcar or hitching to who knows where. But the train doesn't pass by late at night anymore, the schedule must have changed. Or maybe you just don't hear it. Sometimes you talk to her in your head, you say, Ma, come on, things can't go on like this, let me go. You understand, don't you? In some versions she cries and says she wants to die but in others she looks down, nods her head and says she knew this time would come, that she's been preparing for it, she's ready and doesn't want to hold you back any longer. But lately you're thinking that even if that did happen, and you really can't imagine her saying it, but say she did, and you could move out, at this point you're wondering whether or not you could really go through with it. You know now that it's not only her or Jack, but you. And so the days pass, only now there's no spring or light at all, and sometimes it seems that the rest of your life will be like this—one long, dark, winter afternoon.

Rosebleeds
August 1988

Exactly one year after Billy's death and now you write saying you think we should meet. You sign your letter 'Kathryn,' but I notice that your name in the paper is 'Kate.' That tells me a lot. See I know a few things, like about your writing for the paper, I mean. I've lived in this town a long time and I know a lot of people. You say you pass me on the street sometimes and want to stop and talk, that you think we could help each other, that you'd like to be friends. "After all, I loved him too."

Love. You don't know the half of it, you with your words. You don't know about a mother's love for her child; you don't know how much I loved Billy, how much I bled with Billy, and him being what they called then a blue baby; you don't know that after Billy my childbearing years were over—at twenty-four. I had Jack at nineteen, a year after Tony and me were married; then came the two miscarriages, both boys. All my pregnancies were difficult, but I kept on because—oh God forgive me not even Tony knew this— because I so wanted a little girl for my very own, a daughter. But it was Billy that came out, just under five pounds and needing air; so much blood over the white sheet, and me so pale and white, too; red and white, the colors of my life. The doctor told Tony that another pregnancy could be life-threatening, so we had the hysterectomy.

And poor Billy dead now, only thirty-eight. My youngest and most precious—murdered. Sometimes now a picture'll

come into my head of him spread out on the floor of that
damned liquor store, dead white and covered with blood—I
just have to shake it off; oh God in all His mercy!

You write that just a couple of days before his death you
and Billy had talked of wanting me to know about the two
of you, and that you were planning to have me over for
dinner, that you had told Billy you wanted "to meet the
woman who had produced such an unusually sensitive man."
Well don't think you had anything over me, girl; I knew all
right. Billy didn't know that I knew, but I did, and I tried to
keep my mouth shut, until finally I *had* to say something. So
without being too specific I just told him I didn't like him
staying out so many nights. But what I would liked to have
said was, "what do you need *her* for?" Always slinking
around in those black stockings and tight short skirts. Tony,
Billy's father, would never have married me if I'd behaved
like that. He was such a gentleman, and he expected a lady
to be a lady.

Your letter burns in my hand. You tell me how hard the
past year has been for you. What do you know about hard?
You've still got your youth. And I'm sure you must make a
lot of money writing for the paper. As for me, it's a wonder
I get up in the morning, but I do. I get up, put on water for
coffee, and while that's getting hot I put on my face; after all
these years of practice I can do a good, professional job,
fast. It's important for me to always feel ready to confront
whatever might come my way. After the make-up and that
first cup of coffee—that's the best time of the day—the rest
is all downhill. It's a woman's duty, something you probably
wouldn't know anything about, to get all fixed up, *particularly* when her man is gone. And Tony always liked me
best that way.

I was eighteen when we got married; Tony was twenty-
eight. I weighed ninety-five pounds then. Now look at me:
I've ballooned up to one-hundred and thirty-three, which is

plump on a girl five foot two. But who cares, right? Tony did. My Papa knew Tony's Papa from growing up in Brooklyn together.

Those first few years when Tony was working in Arty's restaurant; he'd come home at night—I would have fed the boys and put them to bed, and I'd try to have something special for him to eat. I'd have on a red dress—I had so many of them back then; Tony always said he liked the red against my pale skin, with my jet-black hair. So he'd sit down to dinner and that's when we'd talk. Later, after he showered, and this was all hours of the night, I'd put something on the phonograph—Tommy Dorsey or Duke Ellington—and we'd dance and look at each other and I'd think how lucky I was and remember the first time I saw him.

Our Papas arranged the whole thing, you know, Mama was already gone by then, died so young—and oh!—I rushed around and put on a light pink, crepe dress; I was only seventeen and didn't have anybody to help me or talk to me and tell me what to do, which is probably why I always wanted a little girl of my own—to do that for her. Papa was wonderful, but I mean a woman, another girl to tell you all those things a girl needs to know; my sister Sophie was way too young. Then, when I laid eyes on Tony: "Rose, this is Tony Cavatelli," oh, I just knew! He was so handsome, so tall and strong, with shiny black hair and white teeth; and the way his eyes looked so deep and sad; Billy had Tony's eyes. "Hello, Rose." This handsome stranger handed me a red rose and that was it, I knew that was it—the way a woman knows these things. It was magic. Papa liked Tony, too, but I felt so weak and funny standing there between the two of them, Tony and Papa—like I was being split in two.

So it wasn't six weeks after that before Tony asked me to marry him, and then two months later we did. We didn't need time the way you kids today think you need it. If you need that kind of time then you're not with the right person: you either know it or you don't. So Tony put a down payment on this house—he was proud to be able to do that—and we moved in. Papa was rightfully impressed. And I had so much to learn, like how to cook, which I never did, really—I'm still not good at it; for hot meals I ordered out a lot. But I did learn how to put on make-up the way Tony liked it—from an article I saw by Dorothy Lamour in some high-fashion magazine; and I always kept my hair jet-black for him. Still do; but the only red I wear now is the red of my lipstick.

At least Tony saw his first grandson; Jack and what's-her-name got married in 1973 and didn't waste any time. But then it all comes to Tony dying in '75. He was fifty-eight, and we were *so close* to having enough to get out of the liquor store and buy the restaurant—that was his dream. He worked himself to death, that's what it was. He said he wanted to see me have everything I wanted. So much hope gone up in smoke.

After he died I went on. What else can you do? But I don't hope now, I'll tell you that. I try to be realistic. And, I've tried to live up to Tony's memory, to be Mrs. Tony Cavatelli with dignity.

Look it: three of my four men gone: Papa, Tony, and Billy; I don't count the two that didn't live. Only Jack left, and he'll soon be gone, too, the way he's drinking. Jack looks like Tony, whereas Billy always looked more like me, small-boned. He was such a sensitive, fragile boy that I clutched him to me; I didn't think I could stand losing any more. I can still remember how scared I was when—I think he was around five—Billy started having little nosebleeds. He'd wake up in the morning and there would be these rosy splotches on the white sheets and a trail of dried blood, like a snail might make, between his nose and his lips; or I'd find him standing in the bathroom in the middle of the night, crying, his dark red blood dripping all over that white tile. At first, he was scared too, but after a while he learned that all he had to do to make it stop was tilt his head back, pinch his nose together and then dab it with a tissue. Meanwhile I'd stand there scared half out of my wits and trying to hide my fear from him. I'd seen enough blood already; I was always so afraid of losing Billy. And now I have.

And I'd got so used to having him with me—I guess I thought he'd be here until I died. Of course there was that time a few years back when he had to move out into his own place, you probably know all about that; I think he needed to prove to himself that he could do it. So I just let him go, but he couldn't stay gone for long; he was a homebody. Even back when the boys were young, when Tony would ask Jack and Billy to a ball game or something, Billy never wanted to go. He'd stay here with me and we'd watch TV or play cards, just like we did, well, more-or-less up until when you came along; it's a good thing I've always liked Solitaire. So I don't need you to tell me how special Billy was; I'm his mother, I was there as he was growing up. I watched him and his reaction to things, like how he always responded more to the women in movies than the men. I think Billy was what they called back then a woman's man, as opposed to a man's man. Which is not to say he was a Mama's boy, no, not at all, not on your life! I can still see him sitting there watching old movies with me on the TV, straddling his big stuffed dog—his fine, black hair and pale skin—in the blue TV light. I think he was too delicate for this world. Maybe that's my fault; Tony was always worrying I'd turn Billy into a sissy, which didn't happen, and thank God, Tony lived long enough to see that—he even said it, leaned over and kissed me one night in bed—near the end—and said he thought Billy had turned out "all right." My nights are so lonely now without Billy; he was my companion, after Tony went. He was always such a good boy. Too good, maybe.

And I'd always thought he was happy. But I don't know; I just don't know anymore—about anything.

Like Sophie says to me recently, she says "why don't you remarry, Rose—you're still pretty." I want to slap her, but I just say "Ahh!" and raise my hand like I'm going to. How can she say that? Life ended with Tony. To remarry now would be like digging up his grave and driving his remains through the center of town in a bright red convertible. Then she says she thinks I should get a job working in a beauty salon. But I haven't held a job outside of this house my entire life. I'm just biding my time and hoping the money holds out. There's Jack and his boys, but, to tell you the honest-to-God truth, I'm soured on everything. God bless Sophie, though: surrounded by all men, I've *needed* a woman to talk to.

Why did it all have to end up this way? Maybe it's God's punishment. Maybe I wanted too much, I don't know.

I know I'm not much of a letter writer and that you didn't bargain for all you got here, but just one more thing. You say you feel like we're related, like I'm your mother-in-law or something. But I'm not; the law has nothing to do with it, at least as far as I know. Maybe it does though; maybe you and Billy got married for all I know. What I do know is that I'm not ready to see you yet. Maybe I will be after another year's passed; maybe not. Just don't expect too much out of life, that's what I've learned. And that's what I want to say to you now, Kathryn: *don't expect too much.* Not from me, not from anybody. That's from me to you.

Killing Time
July 1987

Billy stands at the register and glances up at the clock; it is five p.m. Six more hours. He wonders how long he can go on like this, day in, day out. Though he just came in to work at three, it seems as if he's been here six hours already. He hates working cashier and usually doesn't have to, but old Irene has called in sick. He punches "six" and "total" into the register, muffles the sound of the opening drawer with his hand so big brother Jack in the stockroom won't hear, then closes the drawer quietly.

The place is empty, a rare moment; the late afternoon sunlight pours in through the storefront windows, partially flooding the three aisles. Colorful bottles of Galliano, Grenadine, Crème de Menthe and other liqueurs sparkle in the sunlight, dazzling Billy as he stands at the register shielding his eyes. This must be what California is like, he thinks—glittering, all colors, bright, tropical colors and blue sky. Kathryn has said they will go to California together someday; she has described her favorite spot on Stinson Beach, just north of San Francisco. Billy pictures them as they lie across a blanket on the white sand surrounded by high, rocky cliffs. They are talking, but because of the pounding surf, he cannot hear what they're saying. Usually so pale, both of them are tanned and healthy-looking. They smile at one another, get up and race into the ocean, splash around, then run back, flop down on the spread and roll into

each other's arms. The tide washes in, touching the tips of
Kathryn's toes, then ebbs, and as the water rushes back out
and merges with the vast sea, Billy's vision blurs; he loses
sight of him and Kathryn, shakes his head. His mother would
never allow it; he's sure she must know about Kathryn,
though all she has said is that she doesn't like him staying
out so many nights. But Billy feels defeated nevertheless,
and thinks he should just tell Kathryn it's over,
which—though dreading it—he thinks he will do tonight.

Gazing out at the store now, Billy views the three aisles
as he never has before—as the three paths of his life
stretched before him. His life with Kathryn is to the right;
and in the aisle to his left, toward the back of the store, in
shadow, is his brief time with Liam. He wonders now, as he
often has, where Liam is? Such a shame, so embarrassing
the way it ended, his fault, too, after how intense and good
things were between them. But what could possibly have
come of it? They could never have survived together here,
in this environment. Billy pictures him and Liam sitting on
the sofa in Liam's apartment on a rainy Sunday afternoon,
drinking coffee and watching a Greta Garbo movie on TV;
he sees them on a sunny day, shooting hoops at the court on
Appleton Street, or walking along the railroad tracks after
sunset, balancing on the rails and falling, falling, falling into
each other and laughing. But these are all real scenes from
the past; Billy cannot imagine a future with Liam. It is not
Liam, he knows, but a failure of his imagination; or, it is
simply how things are, reality, and he accepts it. Billy
imagines Liam now somewhere in Ohio, his home state, sees
him standing surrounded by golden wheat fields and rolling
hills of brown, rust, ochre, and just a dab of green. That's
Liam: refreshing, undaunted . . . himself; he would have
gotten on with life.

Billy turns away and looks out the window into the parking lot, but sees only the fin of a car and its brightening red taillight before the sun temporarily blinds him. When he turns back around, the store is dark. Slowly, peripherally, as if burning around the edges, the familiar furnishings and objects of the store are illuminated and take shape. There, in the center aisle, stands his mother, Rose. Her arms are outstretched and the palms of her hands are pressed against the opposing shelves, as if to keep them from caving in on her. She looks tired and bedraggled, but perfectly coiffed and made-up nevertheless. As she stands there holding up the shelves, Billy looks at her, watches as the bottles begin to shake and quiver, then rattle and clink. The shelves lurch, teeter, and some of the bottles begin to topple over. Glass sprinkles through the air and the many colors of thick liquor rush out and splash onto the floor, run down the aisle and form a sticky, clotted pool at Billy's feet. He turns to move out from behind the register, tries to run in the direction of his mother, to save her, but he finds himself stuck, his feet won't move; he falls over and out of his shoes with the effort. Suddenly, all the bottles and shelves stop shaking and the store is quiet; Billy looks up to see his mother still standing.

Shrugging out of his vision and looking around, Billy thinks of the one other path, the one final choice or possible exit (besides the back door, which Jack guards): the front door. But that's an option he's had all along, one he thinks about often—just walking out the door and running, running away and not stopping until he can't run anymore, then jumping a train. But to where? And to what end? Or, he could kill himself. But he has rejected that as the wrong way out a long time ago. He wonders if he'll ever leave his mother; she needs him. And just then he remembers the image from moments ago when she stood in the center aisle, or, as he'd last seen her, at home, a few hours earlier, sitting in the corner chair, bending over, painting her nails under the lamp, the light falling into the creases of her face. So sad. She'd had a hard life; she deserved better.

Billy jumps as he hears the bell ring; the door opens, closes, and a customer walks in. But it's only Harvey, a regular, a friendly alkie who lives across the street. Billy nods and says "Yip" to Harvey, their greeting to one another, then looks up at the time: 5:04.

"Be trouble tonight," Billy hears Harvey mumble as he watches him lumber toward the coolers in the rear of the store. "Full moon."

Billy shakes his head, looks back up at the clock and wishes on the swift, relentless beating of the second-hand.

If You're Going to San Francisco

Many years earlier Carey had seen a photograph of Raymond Duncan, Isadora Duncan's brother, walking down a San Francisco street in the first years of the twentieth century, wearing a toga and sandals, his long hair flowing behind him as he was about to cross a street, passing business suits and bustles. Carey would always remember the picture because Raymond Duncan had looked so fierce, so resolute and uncompromising in his nonconformity; so graceful, and so romantic. That image was one of the things that had brought him to San Francisco from Fort Recovery, Ohio, in the late Sixties. *Of course* he had come to San Francisco. Anyone who knew Carey would have expected it, would have said: *he wants to wear flowers in his hair.* He did. And so immediately had he felt at home that he often wore a crown of daisies bought from a vendor in Union Square; he had lived in the Haight in its last, gasping days of glory.

There, he had met many people, some were still his friends; others, many others, had died. And Carey had done it all, tried everything—grass, hash, acid, smack, crystal, thc, mushrooms, meth—you name it. He had hung out in psychedelic shops in the Haight, had hung out in The Panhandle and in Japantown, had seen Janis Joplin in her heyday. And he had survived! He had actually pulled himself out of all of that, and started dancing.

Living in San Francisco, then, there was always something new going on, and somebody—he couldn't remember who—had gotten him involved in a movement therapy group; from there he went on to take classes in Modern Dance—Martha Graham's style was what was being taught then. The contract-release breathing technique at the center of her movement-theory appealed to the mind/body-consciousness of the times, and to him. Carey had started dancing, however, not for health reasons, nor because of Martha Graham or Isadora Duncan, but because of Isadora's brother Raymond.

Most people would not have recognized Carey as a dancer though, and he liked that. Five feet nine, one hundred and eighty-three pounds, he was big-shouldered, broad-chested, strong-legged, and powerful. He looked solid. But when he moved through the air, his long hair billowed.

Today, the morning of his fortieth birthday, Carey woke up and couldn't face the thought of going into the studio. His body was tired, worn out, his limbs and ligaments frayed. He had been thinking about retiring before he made a complete fool of himself, the way so many dancers did, unable to give it up. But if he didn't go to the studio, as he had gone to *some* studio, *somewhere*, almost every morning for the past nineteen years, what would he do? Not only with the day, but with the rest of his life. Where would he go?

Well, nowhere, everywhere: "Rather let me walk," was the phrase that came to him now again and again. He had been reading *Mrs. Dalloway*, and that was what Peter Walsh, as The Solitary Traveler, had said to himself over and over again, sitting in Regent's Park, staring down death.

This is ridiculous, Carey thought now. It was summer, a beautiful day. And yet he was unable to live in the moment, the present moment. He lay in bed; the morning light lengthened across the white sheets. But all he could do was project into the future, or look back at the past. Besides dancing, there had been only one love in his life: Michael. *All that is over now,* he thought, meaning his love life. *Even if I take up with someone again, it won't be like that; it will never be like that again.*

He put a pillow over his face and rolled over, thought he would try to go back to sleep, to stave off the day, postpone making decisions. As his will began to weaken, scenes washed over him, scenes from the past: walking with Michael through the open-air market around the corner from the apartment they shared, his apartment now. They had just seen a movie. It was a summer night. White lights were strung around the L-shaped, green tent; the air was warm. Michael was wearing jeans and a blue and white striped sailor's shirt. He was looking at peaches. He picked one up and turned it around in his hand. It caught the light. Carey saw Michael's eyes flash and felt such a rush of love for him. There were colors, so many colors! And the lush, sweet smell of ripening fruit—the odor of that moment! Carey watched as Michael took a small brown paper bag and carefully filled it with peaches. He put a finger through Michael's belt loop and walked just behind him; they paid Mr. Sung, the vendor, and went home.

Life is so rarely like that, Carey thought now, *rarely so lyrical.* Michael, dead. The ending horrible. Unfaithful, just once. They had been going through a difficult period and Michael had to leave to go on tour with the ballet company. Then, in New Orleans . . . That was 1983. His death was swift; he lived less than three months after he was diagnosed—Carey repeatedly tested negative—two years later. That was mercy.

"Looks like I'll be the *corpse* de ballet," were the first words Michael had said, arriving home from the studio. He'd gone straight to the studio after his doctor's appointment, "*Corpse*, get it?" He stood beside the kitchen table doing relevés. He was still in his leotard, tights, leg-warmers and a T-shirt, sweating; a torn piece of white cloth was tied around his head. He hadn't come straight home; he'd gone to the studio! There were daisies in a blue vase on the kitchen table. *You're the dying swine, Michael!* The vase was the only thing Carey had brought with him from Ohio. *The black swine!* It was an otherwise perfectly beautiful summer day. *How could you, Michael?* (he was crying now). Michael had just used the white rag to wipe his face.

Rolling over in bed, as if to shake free, Carey knew he had to get up. *Must! Must! Must!* But he couldn't move.

All his life he had been pushed, pushed by his parents, by Michael, and perhaps—it was only fair to admit it—most of all, by himself. But his parents had doted on him, an only child. They had told him he was special and that he could do anything he wanted to do, be anyone he wanted to be, be *someone*. And Michael had constantly challenged him to be better, practice more, leap higher. How had he gotten from there to here? Carey realized that he didn't want to be *someone*. He just wanted to be himself, like Raymond Duncan.

He sat up in bed naked and stared at himself in the dresser mirror; it was smooth and round and terribly perfect. He slid down to the end of the bed and, with his feet on the floor, sat close to the mirror. He was transfixed by his imperfect reflection. He picked up a rubber band off the top of the dresser and pulled his hair back into a pony-tail: there was his face, his forty-year-old face. A little morning puffiness, but still taut. Maybe a little too taut. He thought about all the years of dancing, his neck and facial muscles stretching and straining, for air, light, form—attitude. He thought about all the make-up he had had to wear, night after night, over the years, and the hot lights, and how both the make-up and the heat had tugged at his skin. *Gravity catches up with you.* Instead of looking elastic now, his face looked almost exaggerated, caricatured—like the campy face Gloria Swanson made as the aging silent-film star in *Sunset Boulevard.*

Getting out of bed, Carey thought that he *would* retire from dancing. Wrapping himself in the bedsheet and walking out the front door of his apartment, he was almost certain it would be the right thing to do. *Yes, I will just live,* he thought. *I will be a pedestrian. 'Rather let me walk.'*

Now, walking toward the intersection of Fremont and Market streets, the white cloth rippling in the wind, he was in the moment, entering his fourth decade, these last years of the twentieth century.

Idyll of My Son

I've worked for the Parks Department of the City of Baltimore for the past eleven years—doing everything from
landscape architecture to picking up trash. It's an okay job,
as jobs go: leaves you to yourself. The landscaping is easy
and sometimes even pleasing—playing with all that green
life, watching flowers you scattered the seeds for come up
every spring; it's the picking up of trash that I have to go zen
on.

I pride myself on self-reliance; I don't socialize with my
co-workers. Oh, I talk to them on the job and everything, it's
not that I'm a snob. And we get along. But whenever they
start talking about getting together outside of work, I'm out
of there. I've got too much to do. I don't have time. People
always steer you off your path. There's too much to read
and think about. At five every Monday through Friday I go
home to the studio apartment I've lived in since '81, do
some reading, fix-up a little dinner, take a long, brisk walk,
and then read some more. Lights out at eleven. I get up at six
the next morning, exercise for an hour, shower, read while
I eat something for breakfast; then I go to work.

Weekends are best, since I can just sit in one spot for
hours staring out the window at whatever—a bird, a particular branch. It's like holding something up to the light and
slowly turning it around: I can see it and think about it from
every possible angle—within the limitations of my own

mind—and really come to understand not only its physical but metaphysical reality. "The three requirements for Zen are great faith, great doubt, and great perseverance."

I'm saving as much money as possible so I can move to the country someday. It helps that I like having as few *things* as possible. *Things* and *wants* clutter your life and your mind. "All longing produces suffering." I have a mattress on the floor for a bed, a chair, a kerosene lantern, candles, and some kitchen stuff. My clothes either hang up or are stacked on the shelf in the closet. That's it. I don't have a phone. Don't have a TV. I do own a radio, which I feel torn about; but I love music. (Now *there's* someplace to go—into the intricate world of sound. The Brandenburg Concertos. Listening to them is like being in a sunlit room filled with millions of prisms!) I don't buy books—the public library is close and usually has what I'm looking for. Right now I'm reading up on Eastern religions.

I must have read thousands of books in my forty-one years, at least two to three a week—what I can get from the library. And there's a line in one of them I remember from time to time, something like: we tell ourselves stories in order to live. In the latest story I tell *my* self, I have a son—I'll call him Jacob; Jake. He's six and, unlike me, he's chubby, apple-cheeked, and good-natured.

We are on a road trip, driving from Baltimore to just outside St. Pete. I'm taking him to show my parents. I've rented a car and gotten two weeks off work—we're going to take our time. We'll start out at six on a Saturday morning, armed with a cooler filled with tuna sandwiches, cold drinks, milk; we've got a thermos filled with coffee, a coffee pot, ground coffee, potato chips, chocolate-chip cookies, a couple of pots and pans, utensils, and a road map. (We've also got, which I wanted to share with Jake since they were one of the few fond memories from my own childhood, those miniature, foil-lined boxes of cereal that open out into bowls for convenience.) We've rented a tent and sleeping bags—no hotels or motels for us, we'll camp out along the way. But Jake is not yet excited. Still in his PJs, he's grouchy, says I woke him up too early. His presence in my apartment makes it seem much smaller.

"Okay, Dad," he says, finally willing to bargain. "But if I have to get up this early, we have to go to IHOP."

"That's no way to start a road trip, Jake. We get all packed the night before, get up at five so we can leave at six, and then pull over after ten minutes to sit and eat heavy pancakes for an hour? Doesn't make sense." Not sure that he follows, I bring out the clincher: "Look: we'll get a jump on things, get some momentum going, and then we'll stop at a nice roadside park a few hours down the road and eat some cereal at a picnic table. I bought Sugar-Pops."

Bemused, he looks at me like he's strategizing. "Okay."

The early morning light in the room is kind. I rub Jake's head and then completely win him over by handing him my coffee mug. "Here, have a sip. This'll get you going."

He loves it when I let him drink coffee.

Jake looks a lot like Joe Compton, my favorite kid at the day care center where I worked summers during college. I have a photo of Joe sitting on my lap, poised at the top of a big slide, both of us smiling for the camera before our gleeful descent. He was such a happy, healthy, roly-poly boy, just the way I want my son to be.

I'm good with kids, grew up in a house full of them, all unrelated to me—my mother ran a kindergarten in our home for twenty years. There were the summers at the day care center after that, and since then, a couple of stints as a Big Brother. So I'm neither a fly-by-night nor an authoritarian Dad. I know there's a lot Jake can teach me; I just have to be willing and open. But it's not easy, being an adult.

Jake's been saying he has to pee for a while now. He sits next to me on the front seat strapped into his seatbelt, holding himself and wincing.

"See that, Jake? Picnic site one-half mile. Not long now. Hang on." We're in the Appalachians of Virginia and there's some spectacular scenery.

"Look!" Jake points to a steep drop.

"There's the exit!" I steer off the highway, pull slowly into the parking lot, and roll down my window. The sound of bubbling water greets our ears.

"Hear that? I bet there's a brook back there. C'mon."

I accompany Jake into the men's room. Afterwards, we walk back behind the red-brick building. The air is cool and refreshing, the trees whisper in the breeze, and the grass is still wet with dew; it's not yet nine a.m. And sure enough, winding its way about a hundred feet behind the restrooms, there's a brook. I feel completely overcome with joy.

"I'm so happy, Jake. Are you happy?"

He smiles and nods. "Dad, can we eat breakfast right here by the water?"

We do. And as I hoped he would be, Jake is fascinated by the cereal boxes that serve as bowls; the foil lining is an especially glinty attraction. He wants to save his "bowl," so washes it out in the brook when he's done. I watch closely as he stands on a rock, bends over—holding the small box in his hands, and lets the water trickle through. The sunlight catches the clear water and illuminates Jake's pale little fingers. I can see the blue of his veins, and for what seems an eternity, I am lost in the fact of his vulnerability, worried for his future. But then he stands up and screams: "Dad, I caught a tadpole!"

On the road again, back roads from here on, no highways, I show Jake our route on the map. Balancing the cereal carton filled with a little water and the tadpole in his lap, he screws up his face, says he wants to stop and look at things, that he's sure he could find a real arrowhead if I'd just pull over sometimes. Every narrow, dirt road that veers off the main path interests him. At first I am rigid, resistant, and stick to our course. But then because of his persistence, and because I realize he is right—what's the rush?—we pursue Jake's whims.

Down the first side road is nothing much, just more road, and woods. In spite of myself, I feel my adult impatience rushing to the forefront, but restrain myself from saying anything. ("Do not think of yourself as someone's teacher or someone's predecessor"). And then Jake is vindicated: down the next side road we come to an old shack; outside naked kids are all greased-up and running around; down a third country road is a water-mill.

"We're rewarded!"

"See, Dad," Jake says, as we start making our way back out to the main road.

I want to say, 'Yeah, I see, but we're not going to get out of Virginia today.' But Jake wouldn't understand that; he's not yet thinking about his own mortality, caught up in the speed of time.

We find a campsite just before dark, pull over and immediately set up the tent. It's modern and easy to assemble. Jake says he likes the blue-green color, and he loves driving the stakes in with the hammer.

"How about some supper, partner?" I say, pretending to be a character in a Western.

"What do we have?"

"Same thing we had for lunch."

"Not tuna fish again!"

I nod. "Sorry. Tomorrow we'll have to stop and buy some hot dogs and beans for dinner. We can roast the weenies over a fire. What do you say?"

"Yum! And marshmallows, too?"

"Yep."

The sandwiches are soggy by now, but, with the salt of the potato chips, a cold drink, and the tiredness of the first, long day on the road, taste good. Jake crumbles a bit of his crust into the water for the tadpole. Finally snug in our sleeping bags, we both fall asleep soon after milk and cookies.

The next morning I feel a slight, warm blowing against my face. Opening my eyes, Jake's face is right in front of mine. I groan: "What are you doing?"

"Just watching you sleep. It looked like your eyes were going crazy under there!"

I smile and tousle his fine, tawny hair. "Must mean I was about to wake up."

"Dad, can we have some coffee?"

Coffee. Just hearing the word helps. "Yep. Let me start a fire."

Jake helps me gather branches and twigs and when we've got enough, I throw them into the barbeque pit, along with some newspaper, and stick a lit match to it. For a while, he is transfixed by the flames. I go off into the woods to relieve myself, then get out the coffee fixings; Jake picks some of the daisies that grow wild around the campsite and puts them on top of the picnic table.

"I'm real hungry," I say.

"Me, too."

"I don't think cereal is going to do it this morning. What do you say that after a cup of this we find a nice breakfast place."

"Yep," Jake says, imitating me.

It turns out that Sally's Diner is just a few miles down the road. Inside the screen door a fortyish, top-heavy bleached blonde, Sally herself, greets us. Mechanically saying "Hi! I'm Sally. Welcome to my diner," she hands me a menu. "Sit anywhere you like."

It's small and crowded, but we find a table in the corner and sit down. I peek at Jake over my menu. "What'll you have, partner?"

"Pancakes! Pancakes! Pancakes!"

"Okay," I say, running my finger down the menu, "pancakes, pancakes, pan. . . . Here they are: hotcakes."

"No, I want pancakes, Dad."

"They're the same thing, Jake. Just depends on where you're from what they get called."

"Coffee?" Sally asks, walking up and standing close to me.

"Yes. Please. For both of us."

Jake grins.

She sets a full pot of coffee down on the table. "Ya'll boys know what you'd like?" She's standing real close to me now, and smiling.

"I'll have pancakes!" Jake yells out.

"And a glass of milk," I add, pouring myself a cup of coffee and a half-cup for Jake.

"Okay, cutie-pie," she says, writing on her tab. "And what'll the big boy here have?"

"I'll, uh, have the special."

"Sally's Special," she mutters, writing it down and walking away.

Jake fills his coffee cup with cream and then, holding the mug with both hands, takes a big sip; half of his face disappears as he drinks.

"So after breakfast we'll look for a little store where we can buy tonight's dinner."

He puts the mug down and licks his lips.

"Hot dogs and beans, and marshmallows, remember? And then we'll set off. Sound good?"

"Dad, look!" A boy wearing full Indian headdress has walked in the door with his parents; they're headed toward a table on the other side of the room. "Can I go talk to him?"

I look over. The boy's parents look like reasonable-enough people, so I say, "Okay, but make it quick. Breakfast will be here in a minute."

Jake runs over to the table and I hear him growl "Howdy, partner." The Indian-boy jumps at him with a plastic toma-hawk, smiling. I hear Jake say something about arrowheads when Sally slides up to the table with our plates.

"Watch it, they're hot," she says putting them down. "Where ya'll from?"

"Uh, Baltimore," I answer nervously.

"Oh, the big city." She looks at me funny, then leans close. "Listen, honey, don't let me scare you; it's just how I am—friendly, it don't mean nothing."

Feeling bad for her, and for myself, I smile. "Okay. Thanks; thanks, Sally."

She smiles.

"Jake!" I call.

He runs across the room and jumps into his seat.

I should tell him not to run in restaurants but decide to let it go.

"He's got five real arrowheads, Dad, that he found around here. Can we look some more?"

"Maybe."

He looks with disgust at my steak, French fries and huge tomato slices. "What're you eating, Dad?"

"It's what they call Sally's Special. Some people in the south, and in the west, eat like this for breakfast."

"Yuk!"

Chewing, I point my fork to his plate. "How're your hotcakes?"

He hasn't touched them, but he immediately floods them with syrup, cuts a big chunk and stuffs it in his mouth. "Mmm!"

After paying the bill, on our way out I wink at Sally, who flashes the biggest, friendliest of smiles. "Ya'll come back!"

"We will," I promise, deciding to do just that on our way home.

The sky is overcast and looking threatening when we come out of the general store a few miles down from Sally's; the radio reports thunderstorms on the way. Stocked up with hot dogs, beans, marshmallows and apples for lunch, since we had such a big breakfast, I realize Jake's never been in a real thunderstorm, not the kind they have down south.

"You're in for a real treat, partner."

"What?"

"A thunderstorm. You're gonna love it, Jake. I used to sit at the back screen door of my parents' house and watch the rain pour down, listen to it plop into the big puddles. It'd pour for days!"

His eyes grow big listening to me.

"Or, I'd be in bed, in the middle of the night and lie awake watching the lightning zoom into the room and play across the wall, listen to the roaring thunder. It's really something. You excited?"

"Yeah!" he bounces up and down on the seat.

It rains most of the day, which puts both Jake and me under a lulling, hypnotic spell. The radio's too staticky so we sing our own songs. With the first bolt of lightning and ensuing thunder, Jake tenses, grips the seat and looks scared. But when I say "isn't it great?" he relaxes, and begins to enjoy it—covering his eyes (then peeking) and ears, counting the seconds between the lightning and the thunder, screaming with excitement. He leans way over the seat, his face turning red, and says to the makeshift bowl on the floor in a straining voice, "It's okay, Taddy. It's just a thunderstorm."

A couple of times we have to pull over to the side of the road it's raining so bad, like somebody put a bedsheet of water over the windshield.

"Dad, I can't see," Jake says, rubbing the side window with his sleeve.

Besides the couple of times we have to pull off the road, we stop only for gas and a break or two all day and end up in northern Georgia by nightfall, in the Chattahoochee National Forest.

The rain has stopped, or moved out. We set up the tent; Jake hammers in the stakes with his tongue hanging out of his mouth. He gets a kick out of trying to say 'Chattahoochee.'

"It sounds like a sneeze, Dad: Chatchagoochee. Chattaheechoo. Chat. . . ."

I go through it with him patiently, slowly sounding out each syllable, and then stringing them together. In no time at all he's got it, and in his voice it's almost a song, one I will hear on occasion for the rest of our journey: "Chattahoochee!"

But, in the national forest, trying to camp, we're hard-pressed to find anything dry to start a fire with; nothing on the ground. So I reach what branches I can, then shimmy up a big pine already dry from the wind. And with the newspapers I have on the floor of the back seat, we've got ourselves a fire. I open the can of beans, dump them into a pot and put it on the fire, then cut a couple of palmetto fronds and sharpen their ends into spears, as I'd done growing up. Once we stick the hot dogs on the sharp green arrows, we hang them over the fire. I look at my son in the warm, wavering light of the fire.

"You're fun sometimes, Dad."

I reach out a hand to tickle his stomach. "What do you mean *sometimes*?"

"Well, not all the time. Sometimes you're not."

"I know, Jake."

"Look at how fat they're getting!" Jake points.

The grease from the hot dogs drips into the fire, hisses, and spits.

"Dad, what are Grandma and Grandpa like?"

I think for a few minutes, then smile. "Definitely *not* fun."

Jake laughs, then looks confused and worried. But dinner's ready, and any sounds from our mouths, besides the occasional moan or smacking of enjoyment, are silenced.

By the time we get to the marshmallows—and of course we have to try them every possible way, slightly browned, blackened, on fire till we blow them out—Jake is yawning but very happy. For one last treat, I put marshmallows on each end of my sharp stick, light them in the fire, then stand-up and twirl them around in the dark.

"Wow!"

"Now am I fun?" I say, tickling Jake again.

He giggles. "Yeah."

"That's what the majorettes at my high school used to do during half-time at football games. Our team was called the Seminoles, and the girls would have these special batons they'd set on fire. Then all the lights in the stadium would be turned off and they'd twirl in the dark."

Jake yawns again. "Dad, can we look for arrowheads tomorrow morning before we leave."

"Sure," I say, rubbing his hair. "Ready for bed?"

He nods.

"Maybe they've changed," I say to Jake once we're in our sleeping bags.

"Who?" He's drifting off.

"Your grandpa and grandma. Maybe they'll be fun."

He mumbles—something I can't make out.
"We'll probably be there by tomorrow this time."
No response, then the heavy breathing of sleep.

The next morning has that fresh, after-rain feel, and the sky is a cloudless blue. I'm up before Jake, making coffee and thinking. When Jake gets up, he wanders off into the woods to pee, then comes back—asking what'll we do down at Grandpa and Grandma's.

I give him a sip of my coffee. "Oh, I don't know. What do you want to do?"

He shrugs.

"Don't worry, we'll think of something."

"Like what?"

"I don't know, anything you want."

"Um, um—go swimming?—and, and hunt for arrow-heads?"

"You got it."

"But were there any Indians in Florida?"

"Yep. Sure were. The Seminoles. The Osceolas. There were lots of Indians. Still are some."

"Yikes!" Jake grabs his hair.

"It's not like that," I say, and proceed to give him an ab-breviated history of white man's genocide of the American Indian.

"Gee," he says, turning toward the window.

We ride along for a while in silence with Jake looking out his window, and I wonder if I've spoken too soon; maybe I should have waited and let him enjoy his cowboy and Indian fantasy for a few more years.

I reach over and squeeze his shoulder. "You okay?"

He turns to me. "Yeah. It's just sad."

He amazes me! All this time I thought he was feeling sorry for himself.

"Hey look, Jake: 'Welcome to Florida.'"

"Yippee!" He whirls his arm around a few times like he's throwing a lasso. "Chattahoochee!"

"Something real special coming up; I'm going to take
you to the Sewanee Gables restaurant for lunch."

"What's that?"

"Well, there's a famous song called 'Sewanee River?'
I'll sing it for you. And the restaurant is right by the
river—the Sewanee River. I used to stop there a lot when I
was in college. The people who own it are real friendly;
there are heart-shaped mirrors on the wall, and the food!—
they've got the best blueberry pie you've ever tasted."

Jake rubs his stomach.

"You think I'm fun now, Jake, I was really fun back
then."

"Sing it for me," Jake says. And I do.

Sewanee Gables is still the same—the heart-shaped mirrors, the good food and friendly people. We sit at the lunch
counter instead of at a table, right between the two mirrors.
I order our two BLTs, two blueberry pies, milk and coffee.
Jake tells our waitress, an older woman who wears a gold
pin with the name 'Millie' written on it, and the short order
cook, that I used to come there when I was in college. They
both say they're sure they remember me. But I think they're
just being polite; this was twenty-some years ago. I don't
remember them.

The two waitresses fawn all over Jake. It's amazing how
most adults are drawn to kids. Though I know he's special,
it's not just him; it's that adults recognize in kids something
they once had but have lost.

I look over at Jake. He's finished his sandwich and has
his pie and a half-glass of milk in front of him; his hands are
folded on the counter-top.

"What are you waiting for?"

"You. I'm waiting for you! I want us to eat it at the same
time."

I take the last bite of my sandwich and wipe my hands on
a napkin. "Okay, partner, fasten your seatbelt."

Jake and I fork a piece of the pie into our mouths simultaneously and both fall into paroxysms of delight. He squeals.

"Great, huh?"

By the time we've finished, Jake's mouth is ringed with the purply-blue syrup.

"You look like a clown!"

He leans over to look at himself in the mirror and there it is: Jake's face and the background of the restaurant, framed in a heart—a picture for somebody's locket; a picture I'll always have.

I flash my blue teeth at him.

"Oooh," he giggles.

Walking out to the car rubbing our full bellies, I think that we've reached our stride; that it can't possibly get any better than this. I promise Jake we'll take even longer on the way home.

But then the remaining six hour drive passes by so quickly, it's as if we were somehow lifted from the restaurant to my parents' house in a matter of seconds, as if Jake isn't there. And after everything, when we finally reach our destination, my parents' house, I can't envision anything other than this: my father, as always, is at work; and my mother takes one look at Jake, says he's the best thing I've ever done, but that she's tired, sick of kids, and going to lie down. Before she goes, however, she manages to get out the age-old question of why I'm living in Baltimore. I answer, as I always have, that I don't really know, I didn't plan it. After getting out of school I traveled around for a while and did a lot of dumb things—like follow a girl there. When she left, I didn't; that's all there is to it. I tell her I don't plan to stay much longer though, that as soon as I have enough money I'm moving to the country.

But before Jake and I get even the chance to have fun with his grandparents, to hunt for arrowheads or go swimming, my imagination fails me, and I find myself in my apartment, sitting and staring out the window. A Saturday morning, the trees are gray and bare; it's sunny, and people pass by casually, not in a weekday rush. But I *feel* rushed, stirred-up inside, so to calm myself I contemplate the life I'll have in the country someday. I inhale the clean, fresh air, imagine the quiet of the night, picture the stars. . . .

I sit for I don't know how long, fixed on nothing, until a young boy holding a big, blue ball walks up in front of my window, distracting me. He's maybe a year older than my Jake; cute. Then, as if the whole, sun-dappled scene is in slow motion so I can ponder it, he releases the ball into the sky. His red-and-white-striped shirt rises and his small head tilts up, watching, then falls, slowly, as the ball descends; the sun catches his white teeth, and his arms embrace the blue sphere.

Forcing Forsythia

The winter had been much too long and Eli was blue. It was the end of March, spring on the calendar but still January outside and in his heart. He'd moved to Providence from Charleston last fall to take a position teaching freshmen (an *improvident* move, he sometimes joked with Mina, his former advisor in graduate school—at another college down south—who had helped him get the job). Adding to Eli's ongoing funk was the fact that for the first time in seven years, he was alone.

He had given Ben fair warning, remembering now (as he looked out the window onto his narrow, dingy, snow-covered street) that as far back as a year ago he had told Ben, after the latest job offer and subsequent refusal on Ben's part to move, that at some point he, Eli, would simply have to force himself to go: there were no teaching jobs for him in Charleston, nor did it look like there would be any in the near future, and he only hoped Ben would follow. It was late on a Saturday morning and they were sitting at the kitchen table, finishing breakfast. Eli recalled how sunny and warm the room was, and the smell of the special cinnamon coffee Ben always made. He could picture the new green of trees and bushes shimmering just outside the windows, the profusion of color: the yellow daffodils lining the small, rectangular yard visible out the pantry window; the pink and white dogwood trees; soon there would be lilac. It was a year ago, he remembered now, connecting the time with a specific job possibility; it was spring and everything was in bloom.

Eli looked out the window again onto the bleak, metallic, characteristically *northern* landscape, then back at the stack of composition papers on the table; there were sixty-seven of them to grade. But he couldn't do it; he missed Ben.

How two people balanced pursuing professional careers with a love relationship Eli didn't know. Mina had picked up several times, had moved back and forth across the country, bringing the man in her life at the time along. She had a way about her. It was not that she was coldly career-ambitious, but warmly persuasive, he supposed, to her ex-husband and to those lovers who had followed. Why couldn't Ben have followed him? He had often pictured the two of them together, here, in Providence. Sometimes it was a happy fantasy, but other times he could just hear Ben complaining about the weather and blasting him in general for the move. A freelance carpenter, Ben had finally established a steady business.

"You know how long it's taken me to get this thing off the ground," he'd said. "I can't leave Charleston."

"Why?" Eli persisted.

"Because," Ben threw his arms out and looked around the room as if waiting for an answer. "Because I like it here. I'm *from* here; I'm a cracker. You know that." He paused to calm himself, to breathe, then proceeded: "I can't, Eli—it's practically a moral issue for me."

"Whistling 'Dixie' again," Eli said sarcastically; these were not good reasons as far as he was concerned. An Army brat who had lived in nine different cities by the time he graduated from high school, some of which he'd even liked, Eli had never felt attached to a place.

"C'mon in here." Ben beckoned Eli towards the attached garage that served as his workshop. He stopped beside his workbench and rubbed his hands over an ash headboard he was working on. "Surely you don't expect me to give this up; it means just as much to me as teaching does to you."

Eli watched his lover's hands glide across a curve in the design and felt something akin to jealousy.

"And now I'm finally getting paid for it," Ben said, walking out of the room.

They had gone on and on. So where did things stand between them now? Eli wasn't sure. He and Ben had spoken several times since the end of August when, on Eli's final night in Charleston, Ben had avoided him, avoided saying goodbye, by staying out all night and way past noon the following day, "at a friend's," he had explained later. And it had been awkward between them since, when they talked, though it was becoming less so with time; Ben was still living in their rented house. "Alone," he told Eli. Neither of them had yet trespassed outside the boundaries of the relationship. But how long could that last?

Eli looked around the apartment at all the books on the shelves, rows and rows of them, their spines turned to him like an angry friend's back. How difficult they had been, because of their sheer number, to transport. For this, for his passionate love of literature, he had left Charleston, and Ben. And now here he was, teaching eighteen year olds how to write a coherent sentence, building up to paragraphs, and then—glory be—essays: what a wonderful life! But when he connected with even one student, and that student eventually wrote a perfect sentence, it was worthwhile. And his hope, which Mina said was likely, was that a year or two of this would lead to better classes, literature classes.

Mina had been great. They had lunch together almost every Monday, Wednesday, and Friday, when both were at the university. And sometimes on weekends they'd take Mina's nine-year-old daughter Emma, a bright, golden-haired girl who preferred the company of adults, to the movies, then back to her place, or to his, and make dinner; Mina was trying to get over a love, too.

He looked out the window again, then onto the snowdrift of papers awaiting his attention. He needed to get out; he didn't want to be alone, and he thought of calling Mina. But this was a Thursday, one of her two weekdays off, and she was probably at home working on her book; he hated to interrupt her.

Both of them had acknowledged years ago, shortly after he became her advisee, that each felt they'd found a soul-mate, a lost sibling, in the other. What originally drew them together, or rather what brought Eli to choose Mina as his thesis advisor—what, in fact, deepened and made substantial their friendship—was their similar approach to art. Both he and Mina had a background in aesthetics, both had read and been influenced by Susanne Langer's *Philosophy in a New Key* and *Feeling and Form*, and both had the good fortune to be inspired by a philosophy professor who believed in an objective, methodological system by which art could be evaluated. Also, both of them preferred art in which the artist's hand, the artifice—a self-conscious aesthetic—was visible.

Wrapping himself up in an afghan thrown over the back of the sofa, Eli continued to look out the window (it had begun to snow again). He recalled one of his and Mina's earliest meetings in her office in which they resoundingly trashed the "dirty realism" so fashionable in fiction at the time. Besides feeling completely uninspired by the humdrum style, Mina had said she felt strongly that many of the so-called dirty realists condescended to their characters, and nothing raised her ire more than people being robbed of their dignity.

There was nobody like Mina, Eli thought now, turning his mind to consider her good qualities. She was so passionate (so Lawrentian, he and Mina would say), so smart, so full of *joie de vivre*. But equally important to him: just beneath the surface was a vast field of sadness; Mina had experienced far more than one person's share of tragedy in her forty-five years—friends and lovers dead to accident or suicide much too young. Sometimes she was over-burdened by the weight of it all, and Eli had to throw her a lifeline. But today was different. *He* needed *her*. He had to call her. She had said to—whenever; she would understand. And so he did.

When they met for lunch, at a favorite café close to campus, Mina told Eli she had been trying to work on her book but that she was happy to get out of the house, and to see him. "Always," she said. Then she confided that Sven, her most recent ex, had called her earlier that morning. She said it had been a very upsetting conversation and that she'd wasted half the morning crying. Sven had told her she was too old-fashioned for him, and that she doted on Emma too much. She told Eli she'd realized both were true, to which he shook his head. "I almost called you," Mina said, taking a sip of her tea. Then, switching the focus, she asked Eli if he had talked to Ben.

He said it had been a week but that they had discussed spending some time together after the end of the semester—to see how it went. And from there Eli and Mina launched into the subject of relationships, both specifically and in general, love from A to Z, spending almost all of their time together on this one old and, they agreed, very tired subject.

"And of course I worry for Emma and me," Mina went on. "That we're too dependent on each other." She pushed the saltshaker around the table. "I know I can't always rely on her to assuage the loneliness I've felt off and on since her father and I split up; I need adult company, too. But then Emma invariably gets jealous."

They had been talking for over two hours when Mina suddenly looked at her watch and said she had to go; she had to pick Emma up from school at 3:30. "Want to come with me?" she asked. "We could make it a day: go back to my house, make a fire, play with Emma, make dinner. . . . I know Em would love to see you."

"Sounds good to me."

Mina was a terrible driver; she sped across town, turning the wrong way down one-way streets, veering into the next lane; her mind was always somewhere else. The more time Eli spent with her, the more he realized that Mina's absent-mindedness bordered on a carelessness that spilled over into other areas of her life. She frequently lost things, for example, important things—most recently Emma's report card; she had even, awhile back, misplaced a whole chapter of her book, which she was writing by hand. But today they arrived safely with no time to spare, for just as she drove into the school's semi-circular drive, the bell sounded, and within seconds, there was Emma. She seemed biologically connected to the bell, or at least that was how it appeared to Eli when Emma came running out of the building as if suspended on a sound wave.

"Eli!" she screamed.

Eli opened the door and his arms, enveloping Emma in a hug.

"Can I sit up front, too?" Emma asked.

Mina looked at Eli as if it were up to him.

"It would be fine," Eli said, looking first at Emma, then at Mina, "but shouldn't she be strapped in?"

Mina shrugged. And before anything more could be said, Emma jumped into Eli's lap, pushing against him for closeness.

"How was school?" Mina asked, driving off.

"It was fine, except. . . ." Emma paused mischievously, licking her lips and grinning, "except I told Mrs. Zinsser that the 'Pledge of Allegiance' was *appalling* and that I wouldn't recite it anymore." She said "appalling" with bravado, and Mina explained, amid laughter at Emma's defiant pronouncement, that it was a newly acquired word Emma had picked up listening in on one of her conversations, "a conversation about some of our colleagues, by the way."

Eli laughed. "So what did Mrs. Zinsser say to you?"

"She just said she'd talk to me about it later. But she never did."

Mina cupped Emma's face with her free hand. "Just be careful, E. You know how I told you everyone doesn't share our beliefs. You might find twenty-five overly zealous patriots breathing down your throat one of these mornings."

Emma laughed. "Okay, Mom. I'll be careful."

"Now, onward!" Mina banged the steering wheel with her wrist for emphasis. "Eli's coming over!" She looked at Emma for her good response. "Maybe later we can rent a movie."

"Great!" Emma bounced up and down on Eli's lap.

"What shall we rent?" Eli chimed in, and the rest of the ride was occupied with this question, finally winnowed down to a choice between the ridiculous—Emma suggested *Attack of the Killer Tomatoes*—or the sublime, the remake of *Cyrano de Bergerac*, Mina's idea. (Silently, Eli had been thinking of something 60s and French, a sophisticated, *ménage-à-trois* comedy)

Eli loved Mina's house, a white-brick cottage, very English, almost completely invisible from the road, it was so hidden by trees and bushes. Inside was always warm and bright and cluttered (if also messy), a riot of color; most of the furnishings were what Mina had grown up with, had belonged to her family. After they took off their coats and hung them up in the hall closet, Mina suggested Eli and Emma get the fire going while she prepared a snack for them.

Building the fire required only finding something to use as starter, since three good-sized birch logs were already in place. Eli looked around and spotted some newspapers on the coffee table next to a stack of D.H. Lawrence novels. He pictured Mina sitting there earlier in the day when he called, working on her book, a study of Virginia Woolf and Lawrence to be called *The Moth and the Flame*.

Together, Eli and Emma tore several pages from the newspaper and twisted them tightly, so that when they were finished, the newspaper resembled crescent rolls. They stuffed the twisted paper under the ends of the logs, then stood at each side and applied a flame in synch.

"Presto!" Eli yelled.

"Presto!" Emma repeated after him.

The fire roared.

"Wait!" Emma called, still in her pyromaniacal phase. "I have to light the candles, too!" And so she scampered about lighting each of the many candles set about the living room.

Mina brought in a serving tray filled with cheese and crackers, along with three wine glasses and two bottles of a sparkling raspberry drink. She plopped down in an easy chair before the fire. Eli and Emma followed suit; Eli in a rocker and Emma on the floor between them.

At first there was silence as Mina poured their drinks. Eli thought back to his morning and to the bleakness he'd felt.

He looked out the French doors onto the backyard. No. The cold, gray-brown landscape had no correspondence to how he was feeling now.

Mina handed him his drink, poured her own, and the three of them toasted. "To friendship," Mina said.

"You must have paid a fortune for those," Eli said, gesturing with his chin towards the profusion of forsythia forking at each end of the mantel over the fireplace.

Mina and Emma looked at each other and laughed. "Not at all," Mina said. "E and I did it ourselves."

"We forced them," Emma told Eli.

Eli was confused.

"You just clip some branches," Mina said, "bring them in, put them in water, and before you know it, they're blooming; they think it's April! It's a marvelous deception," Mina clasped her hands together. "A triumph of art over nature."

As always, Eli was impressed not only with Mina's knowledge, but also with her take on things. He took a bite of cheese, a Vermont cheddar, which had just the right edge and saltiness; he felt happy.

"Mom, can I paint?" Emma asked.

Mina nodded, her mouth full. And Emma took off, bounding up the stairs to her room.

"Maybe that's all I need," Eli said now. "Some flowers in my apartment." He raised his glass to Mina and drank.

"You're more than welcome to some of our forsythia branches," Mina gestured toward the backyard. "As you can see," she laughed, "we've got plenty."

Emma descended the stairs with heavy, pounding steps; she carried a large, 2 x 3 pad of paper and, balanced on top of it, several jars of already prepared watercolors.

"Put some newspapers down first, please!" Mina requested.

Emma opened several of the newspapers on the floor behind where Mina and Eli were sitting.

Mina turned back to Eli and gestured toward the stacks of books on the coffee table. "I've been noticing in my reading for the book how Lawrence frequently turns to comments about flowers, especially in *Sons and Lovers*."

Eli nodded; he knew Lawrence's work well. "That's his deep love of nature; it comes," he caught himself and laughed, "it comes naturally to him." He was still sometimes unsure of himself in the presence of Mina's brilliance.

"Exactly," Mina said, nodding. "I was noticing just today in *Women in Love* how the main characters are frequently described in floral imagery." She paused and smiled at Eli, as if for punctuation. "But what I've also become aware of is how, as he goes along, Lawrence's discussion of flowers generally modulates into colors; it's as if he's abstracted the parts of flowers that have really been the emotional vehicle all along."

She looked over at Emma. "Tell us what you're painting, E."

Emma looked up, a dab of white paint on her chin. "I'm painting flowers! What else?"

Eli and Mina laughed.

"What flower am I, Mom?" Emma asked.

"You," Mina said, pausing momentarily, "are a daisy. A proud daisy: smart and innocent, golden at the center, but mostly white."

Emma beamed.

Eli looked at Emma thoughtfully. "Martha Graham said 'innocence has the quality of white because it's all-absorbing.'"

"Oh, I love that," Mina said, fingering Emma's golden curls. "So true. You'll have to write that down for me."

Emma tugged at Mina's sleeve. "But Mom, what flower's Eli?" Mina turned back to look at Eli and this time her pause was longer. Finally she answered that he was most like a gladiola.

"What, *funereal?*" Eli laughed.

"No," Mina said, screwing up her face. "Tall and lean. With strong inspirational flourishes."

Eli blushed.

"I think Eli's just an old weed," Emma said, standing up, hands on hips.

"Emma!" Mina cried. She brought Emma's face to hers and whispered "Be nice!" then gave her a love-pat on her bottom. Red-faced, Emma smiled at Eli and returned to her painting.

"I've always considered myself a mum," Mina laughed, picking up the conversation where they had left it. "Something hearty but not uniquely pleasing to the eye."

But Mina was pleasing to the eye. She had an open, generous face framed by light brown hair, a rosy complexion, and moody blue eyes. Eli thought of her as some kind of prairie flower.

"No," he said now, wanting to rescue her from mumdom. "You're something fresh and wild—a cornflower."

"And Ben?" Mina asked.

"What?" The name was far from Eli's mind.

"Ben. What flower is he?"

Eli looked pensive; he took a full minute to answer. "A rose," he said sadly, looking down. "American Beauty."

"Oh, Eli," Mina reached out to comfort him.

"Complete with thorns," Eli added, laughing.

And so the evening passed, *in a roseate blur*, it seemed to Eli when he recalled it later that night. It was as if he'd been drunk. Or dreaming.

The next morning, Eli had to get up early to grade the composition papers he'd ignored the previous day. But he felt up to it, he was restored; the sun was out. He made a pot of cinnamon coffee, then settled into the easy chair with a large mug and the stack of papers. Around eight, he took a break and, simply because he wanted to, perhaps also out of guilt, he called Ben.

"I thought maybe I'd catch you just getting out of the shower," Eli said when Ben answered, sleepy-voiced.

Ben laughed. "As a matter of fact, I'm standing here naked as a jaybird."

"I'd buy tickets to that," Eli said; he always enjoyed Ben's southernisms.

"No purchase necessary," Ben said in a jocular tone. "I'm a freebie. Just come on down."

They had one of their easiest and most spontaneous conversations since last August. And half an hour later when Ben said he had to go, that there was a certain bentwood rocker awaiting him, they had decided that he would visit Eli for three days that weekend.

Both the weekend and the week ahead now looked much different to Eli than they had before his call; instead of looming, they beckoned. He kept atop his classwork, both preparation and grading, and scurried around getting the apartment in shape. He saw Mina again that Monday, four days before Ben's visit, when they had lunch together between classes. She seemed genuinely happy for him when he told her about Ben's visit; she had always liked Ben, she said now. But Eli had always felt tense when the three of them were together, and he realized it was merely Mina's wish to like Ben and for them to get along; whether or not it was true was something else. Mina sometimes had a tendency to put her own spin on things, to see people or situations the way she wanted them to be, instead of how they really were. Eli knew she meant well, and he found this penchant of hers deeply moving—on an ideological level; it was magical realism *applied*, and he had soared on the wings of her good wishes. But experientially, he had begun to feel that this inclination of Mina's sometimes distorted the picture.

"How long can he stay? Mina asked.

"Just three days," Eli answered with something of a wince.

"Well," Mina tossed a hand out in a throwaway gesture. "You might not be interested; you might want to spend the whole time alone together," she smiled. "But just for the record: Emma and I would love to see the two of you, if you feel like it."

"I'd like that," Eli answered. Or at least he wanted to like it, wanted to try. "I'll mention it to Ben and let you know Saturday—if that's okay?"

Mina nodded.

Ben arrived by cab at Eli's doorstep around 9:30 Friday morning carrying a large bouquet of flowers. "From our garden," he told Eli. But Eli was unable to take in the flowers because he couldn't take his eyes off Ben. Seeing him now for the first time in seven months, he had forgotten, Ben really was an American Beauty, and, no doubt about it, a charmer. "Hi," he said, taking the flowers. "I can't tell you how good it is to see you."

"You too," Ben said, fighting back tears and squeezing Eli tight. He put down his suitcase, removed his overcoat, and looked around the apartment. "It's small, like I've heard most apartments up north here are."

"Now, now," Eli mock-warned. "Want anything? Coffee? Did you have breakfast?"

"Some coffee would be good. Bathroom?"

Eli pointed in the right direction and then walked into the kitchen. He put the water on to boil and reflected how it felt to be with Ben. Earlier that morning he had pictured them immediately tearing each other's clothes off and rolling to the floor. But it wasn't quite like that. While it was clear they were glad to see one another, they were also somewhat wary. And now in just over an hour he would have to leave for classes, where he would be stuck until three. He felt frustrated, vulnerable. "Hold me?" he asked Ben when he re-entered the room.

After a minute or two in a silent embrace, Ben let go and gestured towards the built-in bookcase behind the sofa: "Nice work." He walked over and ran his hands along the rim, admiring the inlaid shelves.

Eli smiled, moved as he always was by Ben's hands. He would have to leave soon for class; he told Ben he could come along if he wanted, or, they would see each other shortly after three, if Ben preferred not to go. "I'd like for you to come," Eli said, "but I'll understand if you don't want to."

"Of course I want to," Ben said. "I didn't fly all this way to be separated immediately. Besides, I've never seen you teach!"

Eli had hoped the city would put on its best face for Ben's visit (because the ultimate goal, after all, was to lure him here), and now as they began the ten-minute walk to campus, the red-brick buildings, because it was a sunny day, glowed. Eli also noticed how different he felt in Ben's presence; he felt more real: Ben was his mirror.

"I miss you," he said, turning to Ben as they neared the first class.

"I miss you too," Ben said. "I miss so many things. Like, well," he raised his eyebrows, "the obvious. And eating together. And reading to each other in bed at night. George Eliot's just not the same without you."

Eli laughed. He was moved. But he also felt the very ground beneath him go wobbly, felt threatened. They were on campus now and nearing his building. He knew he'd better lighten things up, quickly shift the focus. "Read anything good lately?"

Ben shook his head. "Not really," he said. "Forster's *Maurice*, which is nothing much. I've tried, but like I said. . . ."

"Well, here we are," Eli interrupted, nervous, as they entered the Humanities building.

Later, over an early dinner at what Eli considered the best restaurant in town, a small, French-country place Mina had taken him to his first few days in the city, Ben said he was impressed with Eli's performance in class. "The way you successfully straddled that very fine line of not seeming authoritarian and yet maintaining control; bringing out the best in them. Just like a well-mannered Southern boy."

Eli smiled, nodding.

"And the students seem respectful of you, not intimidated or, worse, contemptuous." Ben also said he couldn't help notice that Eli seemed completely at ease, seemed to be in his element.

Enjoying their appetizer, a paté with a spicy honey-mustard sauce, along with French bread and a bottle of Burgundy, Eli was pleased at Ben's observations. But he was also increasingly troubled by the inevitability of their conversation. "So where does that leave us?"

Ben put down his fork and reached for Eli's hand. "I want us to be together."

"So do I," Eli answered, withdrawing his hand and silently wondering how teaching and Mina and Emma fit into this scheme. "But how? Where?"

Ben looked down, pushing the paté around with his fork, "You know I can't leave Charleston."

Eli felt the old anger flaring. *Won't leave Charleston*, he thought. And he also thought of the word *inflexible*. But he said neither. "And I . . ." He caught himself and stopped. A busboy had approached the table to clear it in preparation for their entrees. "We're back where we started," Eli whispered as the young man walked away. "Let's not do this. Not now."

Ben nodded. And though they agreed, though both of them wanted to put the issue aside for now, it had them in its grip, so that despite their best efforts, they spent the rest of the meal and the entire walk home either in awkward, false attempts to discuss "safe" subjects, or in silence.

Back at Eli's apartment, however, everything seemed to converge all at once: the seven months of separation; the anger; the lust; the sadness; the tension; the love; the celibacy. . . . They were at each other almost immediately once inside the door, just as Eli had pictured them. They tore at each other's clothes, popping buttons and ripping cloth, until they were naked and entwined on the living room rug.

The following day, Saturday, Eli and Ben slept late and in each other's arms, made love again even before their first cup of coffee, then they prepared breakfast; it was as if they'd entered another time zone. Eli had the presence of mind to mention Mina's invitation, and Ben, trying hard to put his best foot forward, reluctantly agreed. Eli called Mina very briefly to set up plans, then returned to Ben. They talked about everything—Charleston, the house, Ben's business, mutual friends—everything but the future. They made love again, then had lunch. During lovemaking, Eli—

for the first time in their relationship—was the more domi-
nant of the two. Eli could see that Ben was ecstatic, if
somewhat surprised; and Eli found he enjoyed this new role.
For the rest of the day and night, a Nor'easter blind-sided
the city.

The next morning Eli and Ben met Mina and Emma for
a late breakfast at a favorite dive, as they had planned. At
first the conversation was like the winter had been: slow to
thaw; Eli watched Mina and Ben regarding each other warily
as they ordered—waffles all around. The table was just as
sticky—with syrup; all four of them were on their best
behavior. Emma finally broke the ice and developed an
unexpected bond with Ben, when she admired the wooden
figure of a dove Ben had carved, painted, and attached to his
key ring, which Ben nervously fingered. Pleased with
Emma's appreciation of his work, Ben impulsively gave her
the figurine.

"Bird of peace!" Emma proclaimed.

Eli took this as an omen and was grateful, if also oddly
jealous; and he felt some relief in the fact that Ben and Mina
seemed to be carefully skirting discussing anything, anything
at all, having to do with the future.

Afterwards, the four of them walked around the campus,
sloshing through the newly fallen snow—eight inches had
come down during the night.

"Back home, the dogwood are blooming and everything's green," Ben said, eyeing Eli. Eli looked back at him,
then glanced at Mina, who was looking back and forth
between him and Ben.

"But it must be quite a treat for you to see so much
snow," Mina said. "I remember snow almost always melts
before it even hits the ground in Charleston." She bent
down, scooped up a handful and brought it to her

nose—"Mmmm. It's so fresh." She held her hands up to Ben's nose.

"You're right," Ben said magnanimously, redeeming himself, "it is a treat."

Emma threw herself down into the softness, spinning wildly; she clearly wanted their attention.

"Look everybody, I'm making snow flowers," she called.

She got up and tugged at Ben's coat sleeve; her new friend. "Let's all fall down at the same time," she shouted.

They put their arms around each other and stood, all four of them as one, teetering uncertainly, for several seconds. Then, on the count of three as agreed, they fell backwards— *en masse*—into the soft plush of whiteness.

"Wave your arms and legs," Emma yelled. "We're snow flowers!"

The afternoon sun was sparkling, dancing across the snow-covered field. Eli glanced over at Ben and Mina lying next to him, wildly flapping their limbs; their color was high and they were laughing. "Look, Eli," Mina called out to him, "we're blooming!"

Eli stood up. He wanted to see as Mina did, wanted to see the bloom. But all he could see now when he looked at his friends were the wedged shapes they had paved by flailing their arms and legs in the snow.

The Season of 'We'

We were eighteen, boys becoming men, Peter, Tom and me; it was the archetypal golden summer during which such a passage often mirrors the transition between high school and college, but none of us was sure. Like mature tadpoles (or hopeful frogs) we were, not without parental coercion, attempting to shed our tails, grow our own two feet, and hop onto the murky shores of adulthood. During that hot summer all three of us seemed to vacillate between extreme behaviors of the one and the other, and we eventually came to realize such a transformation was indeed a slippery one. It was that delicate awkwardness on which our threesome seemed to float.

Peter, half-Irish and half-Czech, was childlike, full of himself, and he loved, above all else, being loved. Tom, the youngest child of elderly parents, was loving. And I, who always seemed to be in the middle whenever the three of us were together, loved both of them, which made for a disastrous sandwich. But I didn't know that then.

This was Central Florida, the early-1970's, where eighteen, for most of us, was much younger than it is today. We had met at a group for progressive young Christians. Serendipitously, all three of us started attending meetings at around the same time: the fact that we were initiates together made us fast friends. Though obviously searching for *something*, friendship, some affirmation of what we already believed, or belief itself, each of us was there, at least at the start, for a different reason. Being somewhat theatrical, I was drawn by and soon participating in the weekly skits. Though these sketches were often highly imaginative, the viewer seldom escaped without getting hit over the head with some sort of wholesome moral message, of which I soon grew tired. Ever impressionable, Peter was there under the influence of other friends, (friends he would soon drop). Of the three of us, only Tom was sincere in the pursuit of his faith.

This was during the second wave of feminism when so much of the country was caught in its ebb, and there was a good deal of emphasis, at those gatherings, on the need for the sensitization of men, for which Tom, Peter, and I were the perfect, unformed candidates. In the end, though, the meetings were merely a springboard for the threesome we would become, and it wasn't long before we stopped attending. Tom said he was sure-enough in his faith, and Peter and I didn't much care—especially in the face of the opportunity for the three of us to spend time together.

We were children of middle-class homes, living in three different suburban neighborhoods with our parents and siblings. But all of that—our parents, our brothers and sisters, where we lived, our possessions, our other friends, everything else faded into the background once we met each other.

I can still remember my first impressions of both of them. Peter looked like an angel: round-faced, rosy-cheeked, with curly black hair; he was decidedly cherubic. And Tom reminded me of Pinocchio, (no moral analogy intended), with his long, pointed nose set between close-together, green, feral eyes; he had one of the most perfect bodies I have ever seen. I first saw it, all of it, when the three of us were at the lake we frequented that summer. It was in the middle of the afternoon, hot; sunlight sparkled across the surface of the water. Sitting on the dock swinging our bare feet and talking, about blind faith I think, one of us, I don't remember which, (though it was probably Peter), dared the other two to take off all their clothes and jump in.

Without hesitation and without saying a word, Tom stood up and took off his shirt—his broad shoulders tapered down in a perfect V to his narrow waist; next he removed his jeans, and then his underwear. His buttocks were rounded and firm, like an early peach, and I admired the way the sinewy muscles in his legs worked into that solid roundness as he ran down the length of the dock and jumped, cannonball style, into the water. First Peter, (who still had some of his baby fat but was nevertheless muscular), then I, (lanky), followed, and once in the water the three of us wrestled, laughing, our wet, shining bodies rubbing together.

Our bodies, ripe-to-bursting with youth and sexuality, were a significant, subconscious part of our relating. Though we were still innocent and remained so that summer, perhaps more conscious was our knowledge that we were playing, experimenting; and the tease of release was powerful. One of the ways we let off steam was through massage, which we had picked up at the meetings. We called them back rubs, and we soon came to end most nights together that way, naked from the waist up, wearing only our Levi's, straddling one another and kneading away. How I loved feeling their weight on me, the strength behind their hands imprinting itself on my body's memory.

Another sip of release came through kissing each other— on the lips, which was something Peter had started. All three of us were shocked by it at first, but we enjoyed it and so continued to lip-kiss throughout the summer. Though usually quick pecks, the kisses were occasionally long and hard, and tongueless. Except once, when Peter inserted just the tip of his between my lips. I got drunk on it!

We did everything together—camping, hiking, bicycling; we went to the movies and to a concert or two; we slept on the beach one night (an experience made all the more exciting by the fact that it was against the law). And then there was the huge, open field, off the main road on the way to the beach, about five acres or so. We usually went there at night—it was where we could really let go. We'd race, running as fast as we could, calling out and challenging each other, sometimes stripping off our clothes as we ran, each pushing the other two to run faster and faster and faster through the knee-high grass until our legs couldn't keep up and we'd fall down; or we'd stand in the middle of the field and scream—anything we wanted—at the top of our lungs; or two of us would take the arms of the other and swing him through the air until he was dizzy. And we would play the game Trust, where one of us shut his eyes and fell backwards, trusting that the other two would catch him. I usually had a hard time with this.

One of the things that made our threesome possible was that, oddly enough, neither Tom nor Peter was dating—perhaps because they were both more tadpole than frog, and I, though I did not know it then, was dating them. Nor were there the usual homosexual jokes so typical among boys-into-men. In fact, I remember one late night after eating at one of our favorite restaurants, a pancake house along busy highway 17-92, we were standing out in the parking lot saying goodbye, hugging and kissing as usual, when two men in a rust-colored car with a poor exhaust system drove by and yelled, over their ragged muffler, Faggots! Peter and Tom were kissing at that very moment and I was standing beside them. I flinched at the sound of the dreaded word and backed away a few steps. Though I did not know, for sure, that I was gay, I experienced a spark of self-conscious recognition at the accusation; I had been found out. But I remember so well Tom and Peter's response: they looked at each other, then at me, and burst out laughing! Ever-generous and daring, Tom walked over and kissed me on the lips, and we all laughed again, though I felt jealous of their easy dismissal of the epithet that had been hurled at us. Alone. Then Tom raised the ante even higher, added yet another chip to the kitty of our romance. Looking me straight in the eyes, he said, I love you. It became, then and there, part of our repertoire.

Breakfast was our favorite meal. Whether late at night after back rubs or a trip to the field, or early morning before a jaunt to the beach or a canoe trip down the Wekiva River, or late morning after a late evening and a good night's sleep, we would meet at one of three places, eat breakfast and talk for hours. Religion was our main topic of discussion. Tom—a steadfast and thoughtful believer who always impressed me because he actually used his mind and took nothing at face value—questioned everything and was continually challenging Peter and me. I had difficulty with the concept of faith, because I saw it as being *always* blind. I had never, not once, I said to Tom, seen proof of God's existence; had he? (of course he had). And Peter blew about with the wind on matters of faith, but he was well enough versed in Bible-speak to be able to impress Tom when he wanted to.

As for the other main subject of our conversations, music, we had similar tastes, which tended toward the well-crafted folk song by both male and female singer-songwriters. We analyzed the lyrics for hours, and some-times we sang. In fact, the only time we ever got drunk together, we were sitting on the dock at the lake singing at the tops of our voices. Peter even stood up to better throw himself into the song, his curly-haired silhouette almost black against the spotlight of the full moon.

But then the light, *their light*, which had come to seem as natural to me as that given off by the sun or the moon, went out. On the 15th of August, the day after our drunken song-fest by the lake, Tom and Peter told me that, come September, they were going away together for three months to work at a camp in the Rockies owned by the young Christians organization. We were standing in the parking lot of the pancake house again. Tom did all the talking. He winced and said they had put off telling me—they had known for weeks—because they didn't want to hurt me. Otherwise, he said he couldn't really explain it—it was something they wanted to do. He said he was sorry. Peter just stood there with his head down, nodding; he was gutless.

My cheeks burned. I felt hot. Tears welled in my eyes and my throat constricted. Good Christians! I thought, wishing the two of them were dead. But I couldn't say a word. All of the life and esteem I had gained through my friendship with them seemed to drain out of me and collect in a pool at my feet. I turned away, shielding my face. Tom tried to put his arm around my shoulder, but I shook him off. Somehow, I gathered myself together enough to take off running; I ran as fast and as far as I could, until I was out of breath and couldn't run any farther.

Over the next two weeks, despite repeated phone calls from both of them, and several surprise visits by Tom, I refused to see or talk to either of them—much to the exasperation of my family.

And then they left town.

It rained for two weeks straight that September, and I broke down. I died and came back a completely different person, my chromosomal furnishings seemingly rearranged.

Suddenly, I was dark, introspective. Where I had not been a reader before, I now devoured books. I read all of J.D. Salinger; and these lines from Carson McCullers's *The Member of the Wedding* made a great deal of sense to me:

> They are the we of me. . . . She was an I person who had to walk around and do things by herself.

But I also read heavier, weightier books—*The Diary of Anne Frank, Dear Theo* (Van Gogh's letters to his brother), even Dostoevsky and Kafka.

I did nothing else that fall—didn't look into applying to colleges, nor did I get a job. Instead, I sat in my room and read or looked out the window at the rain; sometimes I took long walks and got soaked. My parents were worried about me, but fortunately they had the good sense to more-or-less leave me alone.

I started keeping a journal and scribbled away in it feverishly. It was there I worked out the many theories as to why Tom and Peter had done what they had, most of which were a variation on the idea that they knew and were embarrassed about my homosexuality, and that they had simply chosen to put some distance between me and them. It was in the pages of that journal where I first began the long, slow process of coming to terms with being gay; and it was there that I continually reminded myself, tried to force myself to look at and accept the hard fact that I was no longer part of a 'we.'

But splitting off from me seemed to kill them, too. Something happened between Tom and Peter that fall which would change their relationship forever, a fact Peter later mentioned rather provocatively, then refused to expound on. My best guess has always been that he told Tom he was in love with him, and that Tom simply couldn't handle it.

I saw them only occasionally after that, when they returned from camp; but it was never the same. And then I moved away—to go to college in Boston, where I have stayed and made a life for myself (with a lover and a good job). Of course I have thought of Tom and Peter on occasion over the past twenty years, but I rarely got past their names, and I wouldn't let myself remember much of the context.

It was the smell of rain which first set-off the memories—the smell of rain when the temperature and the humidity were just right and my mind was loose and free enough; not often. Once the memories started, everything seemed to connect to that time. Hearing Nina Simone sing "This Year's Crop of Kisses," I couldn't help thinking of Tom and Peter, for obvious reasons, I suppose—that year's crop *was* particularly sweet to me. Finally, as if this confluence had been building towards an end, (and hadn't it?), there were some hard facts. A friend visiting her parents in Orlando had seen Peter and Tom. Both are married, with kids; she said they seemed to almost vie with each other in expressing their curiosity about me, plying her with questions and telling her to be sure to say hello.

Only this summer have I been able to allow the memories to come washing over me; I must have been ready. Remembering has been harrowing; sometimes I haven't wanted to return to the present. Not because life is so bad, but because of the heightened intensity of those youthful experiences. Remembering has also reconnected me with some of the happiest moments of my life, experiences which seem so remote and foreign to me now, of another season. . . .

There was a five-story high parking lot in downtown Orlando we occasionally rode our bikes to. Late at night, when the lot was empty, we would walk or sometimes ride our bikes to the top story, and then coast down the declining ramp five floors, feet on our handlebars, wind in our hair.

I suppose we had done it often enough that our enjoyment of it was beginning to pale, so Peter—who else?—decided to raise the stakes this particular August night.

Why don't we try doing it holding hands? he suggested.

It was the sort of exercise in risk and trust Peter thrived on, and which now best characterizes friendship for me.

Tom shook his head and smiled at him, then at me.

Always eager to fit in and be up to whatever challenge or dare the two of them might present, I nodded. I will if you will, I said to Tom.

It was after midnight and the city had grown quiet. Peter just sat there on his bike looking at the two of us, waiting.

It's crazy, Tom finally said, scratching the back of his head. But I'll do it.

We walked our bikes to the top of the lot and positioned them at the edge of the incline. Tom said, If you feel yourself starting to wobble at all, let go, okay? Peter and I nodded. We mounted our bikes. We were nervous. We grabbed hands—I was in the middle and so had nothing to hold onto the handlebars with. I had to trust Peter and Tom with the steering. I felt their firm grips squeezing my hands, felt their pulses and mine beating together, blending. Now, Tom said.

We lifted our feet off the ground and began moving, slowly at first, but very soon we were coursing through the air as one. The corners were difficult, but wide, and we made the first one. Tom shifted his grasp along my forearm to my elbow. We wobbled, but none of us let go, nor did we fall. We couldn't look at each other but instead had to stare straight ahead, silent, Tom and Peter steering with their free hand. We were going faster now, but we made the second corner as well. It's all downhill from here, Tom said, and Peter started laughing.

But Tom was right. We sailed on, down, faster, to the bottom level, exhilarated, still holding hands, still "we."

The Real, True Angel

They called him Angel and always had, the men in his many circles of friends over the years, though his Venetian-born parents, or rather his father—for he was the only one of the two who really cared—had christened him Angelo. But the members of the various circles called him Angel always, and the name was passed on from one group—member to member—to the next; Angel not because he looked "angelic"—his hair was not golden (nor haloed), though it did fall in ringlets; Angel not because he was a benevolent innocent from above (no messenger from God he); nor could his wiry body possibly be construed as cherubic. Instead, Angel's hair was black, a black so black it shone blue in sunlight, and his almost hairless skin was fair—the sheen in his hair somehow picking up on and bringing out the delicate blue veins that coursed just beneath the surface of that marvelous translucent skin. Most of the time he simply looked electric.

And to further disprove any possible corroboration what-soever between name and deed (or being), it must be said that, dispositionally, Angel had an attraction to danger. Nevertheless, the men in the various circles over the years persisted in calling him Angel, and perhaps the easiest

answer to the riddle why (other than the wildfire theory—
that it had caught on, and spread) lay in man's sheer laziness: Angel, because it was an ever-so-slightly shortened
version of Angelo, and thus one syllable less to roll off the
old cow tongue. So Angel it was; the name had stuck. And
the one thing about it which Angel said rang true to him,
though he hadn't realized it until he was in his late 30s, was
the fact that he had never, not once in his life, felt grounded,
of this earth—though he longed to: the unbearable lightness
of being indeed!

> But in the love poetry of every age, the woman (or
> man) longs to be weighed down by the (other) man's
> body. The heaviest of burdens is therefore simul-
> taneously an image of life's most intense fulfillment.
> The heavier the burden, the closer our lives come to
> the earth, the more real and truthful they become.

Angel's age? That was not a simple matter either, but a
subject of some debate. Angel himself claimed, in character-
istic straightforward, no-nonsense fashion, that he was now
fifty-eight, though few of the men in his ever-changing
circle had believed him whenever he'd divulged his age,
thinking that, instead of subtracting years—as most self-
respecting homosexuals and women, and even a few hetero-
sexual men did, subtracting ten or, if they could be so bold,
fifteen, or even twenty years from their true age (this latter
mathematical feat one few but Angel could actually get
away with)—Angel, they said, did just the opposite (as he
had so often in his life); Angel, or so they conjectured,
added years to his age—so that everyone would look at him
and think, and perhaps even say, "My, you don't look
fifty-eight."

But there it was, the unadulterated, undoctored proof, evidence—his Birth Certificate, or "Certificate of Live Birth" as it is still known in many cities and towns through out the South, one copy filed away in the Bureau of Vital Statistics at the State Board of Health, the other tucked away only the devil knew where, now that Angel's father Giovanni had passed on:

Angelo D'Allura, born to Giovanni and Philomena D'Allura, in The City of New Orleans, in the State of Louisiana, in the Year of Our Lord, Nineteen Hundred and Thirty-Six.

But there was Angel's body, they said—for many if not most of those who knew him also knew (or had known) his body, intimately: there was no way *that* could be a fifty-eight-year-old body, so lean and taut and, excepting certain areas of the face—those soft, dark pockets beneath the eyes and the parenthetical marks around the mouth—so smooth and wrinkle-free (nor was his hair graying).

Angel was fifty-eight, he simply didn't look it, though he had certainly and unquestionably and fully lived each and every one of those years (months, weeks, days, hours. . . .) After his first eighteen years, growing up in New Orleans (if such a synonym for maturity could be ascribed to anyone raised in that town), in the Garden District no less, where many of the houses, Angel had always said, looked as if they were made of wooden lace, he had moved to New York—Angel had lived in and known well some of the most cosmopolitan and exciting cities in the world, always searching for home, yearning for a base, a groundedness, a world beneath his feet. From Manhattan, where he'd stayed for the better part of a decade, after which he'd moved— naturally, or so it seemed, to everyone at the time, most of whom had or eventually would do the same—to Paris, where he had felt lightness the most (another decade); from there it was Amsterdam for a couple of years (which he'd soon tired of), then Rome, his parent's native Venice, London and, since he'd been able to avoid Australia altogether (for despite all the brouhaha about Australian men, Angel knew, intuitively, that it was not for him), back stateside in the mid-80s—to San Francisco, to lovely, funky Provincetown, and finally, once again, to a heavier place, "home"—New Orleans, still searching. Which was how—as if logic or fate had played a hand in the unfolding and development of this absurd turn in the events of Angel's life story—how and perhaps why he ended up where he was this very morning, sitting on a cot in a New Orleans prison, his head in his hands, arrested and accused, of pederasty.

The police report alleged that on the afternoon of Friday, June 5 at approximately 3:30 p.m., one Angelo D'Allura lured eight-year-old Sanders Parker, on the way home from his last day of school that year, into the old St. Louis Cemetery, and therein—and for the next hour, hidden amongst the above-ground tombs—committed "heinous sex crimes" upon the boy.

The charges would have been amusing were they not so serious, as anyone who knew Angel also knew just how ludicrous such allegations were: for not only had he never favored (or pursued) children—they would never be able to bring him down, weigh him down, to earth, and their minds were not complex enough, he said, for what he liked.

What he liked; his preferences: an *almost*-violent aspect to sex. Not S-m, not theatre of any sort—no *accoutrement* necessary, but an exchange between two men that was nearly vampiric, volcanic, oceanic (name your synonym for size, power, depth), in its fathomless degree of passion and intensity. Sex was successful and thus enjoyable for Angel if and only if the lover left some sort of physical evidence of that intensity on the beloved's body each and every time (it took *that* much for him to feel it and know it was real)—a bruised knee, a scraped arm, a cut, bloodied lip, nose, or ear, a sore, tender, even slightly-torn nipple, a sensitive, swollen cock, a heart murmur. . . .

And so it had come to this—after all the years, all that space, all those cities and all that life experience (*Non, je ne regrette rien*, Angel had often said)—a 12' x 12' jail cell (6' x 6' if you considered the fact that he was sharing it). But as in every city he had ever lived, Angel had friends, friends everywhere, in high places and in low, and he quickly set them to work, searching for an explanation as to what had happened to him and, more importantly, for his key to freedom. Disallowed bail and visitors (except his lawyer), Angel passed his first few days ruminating, remembering, and wrestling with the problem, the question, of who had set him up (never mind the why just now).

That he must have a few enemies in New Orleans, Angel did not doubt, because he knew, too, that the natives did not look kindly upon one who left them, as Angel had those many years ago; nor do Southerners forgive and forget easily, Angel reasoned: witness the Civil War. But who those enemies might be Angel could not guess. A relative, he supposed, would be the most obvious choice, given natural law, but only two remained in the City of New Orleans as far as he knew: His ninety-eight-year-old maternal grand mother Sophia Orioli and his Uncle Luigi, his father's younger brother, who had been drunk for at least the past forty or fifty years; and Angel had seen nor heard from neither of them since he'd left the city in 1954.

*

June 5: Angel remembered the day well. Rain had fallen in sheets all that afternoon, much of which he spent, in the company of another man, ducking in and out of dark churches (as the air smelled of copper and the architecturally appropriate copper itself slowly refined its greenish hue, like a sunbather working on his tan). And then, late in the day, the two of them had entered the old St. Louis Cemetery. Angel closed his eyes now and tried to remember, to picture the scene that day: had he seen anyone, or anything— suspicious looking? Or could the other man, whom Angel had met only that morning, somehow have been involved? No—Angel trusted his instincts implicitly. A friend of the family's then? Angel wracked his brain and came up empty, and it was then that he realized, after several such days of considerable cogitation and aggressive self-questioning in general and more specifically from his lawyer, that for the sake of his mental health he would have to let it go, to leave it to his lawyer and to his friends to resolve. Looking around his cell now, at everything that was cold and sterile—the iron bars over the ice cube of a window (with neither green nor blue in sight), the metallic, lidless toilet, the creaky cots, even his cellmate was cold (pale and hairy)—Angel knew that if he was going to survive this, he would need to dream. . . . And, he told himself (intuition?) that perhaps a trip back in time would also help him discover how he had arrived at where he was, and who had sent him there.

*

Because he had had so many lovers and sexual experi- ences in the almost-forty-five years he'd been a player (yes, Angel had long sung the body electric!), his memories of those lovers and experiences—for those were the dreams he turned to now—were fractured, cinematic, but there were a few scenes he could remember vividly.

Angelo, as he was still called then, was thirteen when he lost (or *gave* would be the more appropriate, *active* verb) his virginity; it was during that still-exuberant, burgeoning time in American history between the end of WWII and the beginning of the silent, lobotomized 50s.

They had just met, Angelo and his man of choice, had run into each other amidst the wild roses growing in some rude field outside of New Orleans center, not far from the Mississippi; it was past two in the full-moon summer morning. Angelo, need it be said, was decidedly precocious (Angel sat back and let the screen roll):

Have you ever noticed, he asked the man, his voice still at the cracking stage and *doing just that* (much to his embarrassment), how the texture of rose petals, not these but those of the long-stemmed variety and particularly when still buds, seems to resemble the head of a penis, especially when erect—*that soft, velvety, multi-striated look*? Even the shape. . . . (Angelo was nothing if not verbose in those years, whereas Angel was known for a much more laconic style).

The other man, somewhat older but devastatingly attractive and wearing a crimson tie (a signal to those of like mind back then), a Dirk Bogarde type, seemed caught off-guard with this rather florid display of verbal foreplay, and gave Angelo a questioning, surprised look.

Have you ever eaten one—a rose petal? Angelo went on.

The man shook his head.

They're surprisingly bitter; not at all the pleasant taste you might think.

And then I took the rose into my mouth and. . . .

Sweet memories! The field, it turned out, was well-known for such nefarious activity, and Angelo became a

frequent visitor. For at fourteen he had been inspired—
ignited might be the more appropriate word for what he
felt—by the possibility of a true brotherhood of men, *boon
companions*, one which included sexuality, a utopic dream
brought on by his reading of Whitman ("Twenty-eight young
men . . ." etcetera), D.H. Lawrence, and—much to his
surprise—Melville. In fact, it was the following passage
from *Moby Dick* (dedicated by Melville to his beloved
Hawthorne) Angel recalled now, still able to recite it from
memory, which had set him on his path in life:

> I washed my hands and my heart of it. . . . while
> bathing in that bath, I felt divinely free from all
> ill-will. . . . Squeeze! squeeze! squeeze! all the
> morning long; I squeezed that sperm till I myself
> almost melted into it . . . till a strange sort of insanity
> came over me; and I found myself unwittingly
> squeezing my co-laborers' hands in it. . . . Such an
> abounding, affectionate, friendly, loving feeling did
> this avocation beget; that at last I was continually
> squeezing their hands, and looking up into their eyes
> sentimentally; as much as to say—Oh! my dear
> fellow beings, why should we longer cherish any
> social acerbities. . . . Come; let us squeeze hands all
> round; nay, let us all squeeze ourselves into each
> other; let us squeeze ourselves universally into the
> very milk and sperm of kindness. Would that I could
> keep squeezing that sperm for ever. . . . In thoughts
> of the visions of the night, I saw long rows of angels
> in paradise, each with his hands in a jar of
> spermaceti.

That was the life Angel had first envisioned and wanted
for himself at age fourteen—a fantasy life really—an open,

generous, magnanimous, sensual life in the natural world in which he was a part of and surrounded by a chorus of men. And, it was, more-or-less, the life he'd had.

Doesn't the warm air feel nice on your bare ass?

Another voice. Another experience. Another memory. It was something someone had said to him once, after sex, as they were standing in the weeds along the shores of Lake Pontchartrain, their pants down around their knees; (Angel could remember that the man's cock was as stiff and as long as the tongue in the bell of St. Louis Cathedral, extending a full third of the length of his leg); Angelo might have been sixteen. Such a simple statement—*Doesn't the warm air feel nice on your bare ass?*—but Angel had remembered it always, and treasured it, *because of its simplicity,* its sheer, simple, truth and beauty, its contentment with, and in, the moment—*that the moment was enough.* Somehow, that one sentence seemed to capture or express the very life that he wanted.

*

The next day, awake before the rooster's crow, Angel lay on his cot worrying over the fact that, after a mere three days, the relationship between his cellmate and him, a large, bulky man named Brice (who was still asleep), had begun to deteriorate—not that it had been much good from the start. But this was unusual for Angel, since he generally got along well with people, particularly men—men of all types, and he found it troubling.

All he knew of his cellmate, besides his name, was his number, 406754, and that he was in, this time—his third, for raping his eleven-year-old niece, of which he'd told Angel

that first day: ("Brice, Brice, red beans 'n rice," his sister
had teased him when they were teenagers. Then he'd added:
"Guess I got her back.") Brice had become unfriendly and
downright unkind to Angel—refusing to talk much after the
first day, or when he did talk, it was only to castigate or
curse at Angel for something or other, something as innocent
and involuntary as sneezing, for example. Brice's bullish-
ness and *théatre di machismo* had the unfortunate effect of
seeming to reduce Angel's space in the cell to something
less than negligible. And then it hit Angel: Of course! Brice
must have somehow found out about the charges against
him—*and believed them.*

That same morning, after breakfast, of which Angel only
drank the coffee, black, his lawyer—the Francis Hardin—
and two of Angel's friends, men of the chorus, awaited him
as he was brought into the visiting area promptly at 9 a.m.

"Victory Number One!" the zealous young Hardin said,
arms raised to the skies, his fleshy, white underarms like
some white-bellied fish lost swimming in the loose folds of
his short-sleeves; he was referring to the fact that he had
won the right for Angel to have visitors, two at a time, other
than himself.

Though Angel and his friends were separated by a
wall—half of which was made of concrete and the other half
of a thick, almost opaque plexiglas, even that couldn't
dampen their pleasure in seeing each other. But Hardin
insisted they get right down to business, saying there was no
time to lose. He told Angel that his two friends there had
visited his Uncle Luigi and that Uncle Luigi could confi-
dently be ruled out as a possible suspect: now *that*, he said,
that was progress.

"He was very sweet," one of the men said, looking Angel
directly in the eyes.

"If also constantly drunk," the other said. "It's his *'lifestyle,'*" he added, winking.

"He spoke about your father," the first friend continued, "his brother Giovanni. And about how much Giovanni loved you, his only child—his son, and how he could still remember your father's happiness, the look on his face—how he glowed with pride, when you were born—his Angel."

"And he told us the story about the time when your mother was out of town for a month visiting relatives in Italy. You must have been about seven or eight, he said, and the three of you—Luigi, Giovanni, and yourself—set-up house together, *for the month*. He said he had the both of you drunk and wearing aprons in no time!"

Angel smiled, remembering, and Hardin blushed. What was next? Hardin's body language seemed to verbalize. The grandmother—"the Orioli woman," he finally said aloud, raising his eyebrows and looking away from Angel.

Always quick, vigilant, and perceptive, Angel caught it, that *something*, an evasiveness. "What is it, Frank?"

"What?" Hardin replied, knowing he wouldn't be able to wiggle out of it. He looked down at the floor and muttered: "Advance word is not good on that."

A question mark formed in the furrows of Angel's brow, where it seemed he held an endless supply of punctuational symbols. But before Angel could say anything, Hardin stuck out the palm of his hand—like a traffic cop. "Let's just wait and see," he said. "We've got a couple of people, friends of yours, working on it." And then their time was up.

Left alone once again, virtually, spiritually alone, Angel returned to the arduous, if also ardent task of remembering. But he was tired today, and instead of actively willing his memories, this time he simply let them wash over him.

*

June 5. It was the last time he'd had sex: Angel and *the man*. They'd spent much of the afternoon dancing around each other, so to speak, until finally, what they did together was so tame, yet so fulfilling—just what the doctor had ordered that particular day: *The man* stood behind Angel, his stiff cock between Angel's legs, and fucked him while jerking-off Angel with one hand, the palm of his other hand pressed tightly against Angel's heart, almost constrictingly, so that he was enwrapped; *enrapt*. Someone was practicing the organ in the church at the time, and so it was to that deep purple gothic strain that Angel—by now a connoisseur of the orgasm—came: *And in his mind's eye he saw—in quick flashes—the flying buttresses and the stained glass windows of Chartres, the open-mouthed gargoyles of Notre Dame, and in his ears he heard an aria by Callas. . . .*

Angel had come in endless waves that day it seemed to him now, lapping at the shore of the man who was—at least for the day, the moment—his lover; it reminded him of how—as a boy edging puberty, he had loved to kneel, naked, along the banks of the Mississippi, and masturbate into what little ebb and flow there was.

Such thoughts carried Angel past dinner—a tableaux in which he felt himself to be both the diner *and the proverbial, implattered fowl*—which he didn't touch, and into the night, further into dreams, and finally to sleep. But his sleep that night was fitful and inconstant, as he could not escape the sinking feeling that Brice, and possibly others as well, were watching him, hunting him, hovering over him even, at times—all yellow teeth and matted hair: positively Werewolvian. He heard voices, too, in the night, voices saying something about "Go fish!" Voices seeming to call to him, saying "What's she in for, Brice?" And "Sister Angel,

what you in for?" "I'm gonna be in you for what!" And then
a deep, sinister laughter that tingled his spine.

*

The next morning Angel sipped his black coffee in
silence, sitting in the path of the shaft of soft light projecting
in through the tiny window while Brice continued to sleep
(or pretended to sleep, Angel couldn't be sure). This was
Angel's sixth day in prison, *imprisoned*, and though he had
awakened feeling groggy and tired from the sleepless night,
he now felt energetic and was looking forward to going
outside as scheduled—one hour after lunch: the exercise; the
fresh air; the open space. . . .

That time, too, when it came—like the prospect of sleep
the night before, a seeming respite which proved otherwise—was not what he'd hoped it would be. Oh, the first
few minutes were delicious all right—the feeling of the air,
though hot and humid, on his skin; he could feel it bristling
through the hairs on his arms. The natural light on his face
and on the faces of the others, shading bones and five
o'clock shadow—*chiaroscuro*; and all the colors and the
wide openness of it all. . . .

But before long Angel became aware of a sort-of
collective bad mood among some of his fellow inmates in
the yard, a foulness that apparently had something to do
with him, like a conspiracy. Fortunately, this feeling seemed
to be contained to a group of less than ten men, some of
whom—when they thought they were out of sight of the
guards (or as out of sight as they could be)—pulled out their
penises and mocked jerking-off, taunting Angel, making
pronounced, exaggerated sucking noises as they did so;
others pulled their pants down and mooned him. And a
couple of the larger men walked past him so close that their

uniforms brushed against his and whistled a secret, menacing, non-verbal message, and at the same moment they mumbled, almost under their breaths but not quite, still audible, mumbled some deep-voiced threat like "Just you wait, sister!" and "Pervert!" and "Boy-butt fucker!"

Because the group seemed relatively small and contained, Angel was hopeful; he believed in his powers to tame them, in fact he felt somewhat challenged and excited by the possibility and the danger. And yet he spent the rest of the day feeling as though he were walking in a dark tunnel—*not much space, nowhere to run*; the walls closing in around him; the entrances and exits blocked off. He was trapped; surrounded.

*

"I baked you a cake, honey," said another visiting member of the chorus, a petite drag queen holding out her hands *as if.* It was the next morning and Angel had somehow slept like a baby. Now he was greeting Hardin and two *other* friends.

"But don't you go lookin' for no file," she went on, "cause there ain't one. Ain't because I didn't try, though: Mr. Hard-on here wouldn't let me."

Hardin blushed and pulled at his lapels, which Angel recognized as the opening moves of his trying to take control of a situation. "We've seen your grandmother—Madame Orioli."

Angel said he was all ears. Hardin looked at Angel's friends.

"You shoulda seen Miss Thang," Angel's petite friend went on. "I mean that girl is big, as in *huge*! And old! Honey, you ain't see nothin' that old since the last time you was in Europe. And that place o' hers! Splendid squalor, that's what it is. Splendid squalor! And her squattin' there in that dilapidated Peacock chair o' hers like it was a throne, and with enough chins to make a chinchilla. Why, I couldn't tell where Granny ended and the chair began. Pity that poor, sagging wicker's all I got to say!"

Angel was smiling.

"All right, all right," Hardin interrupted, "Let's cut to the chase." He fixed Angel with a serious look. "She says she's responsible. Voodoo."

"Seems she's been practicing for years," his sober friend chimed in. "And recently, well, after Giovanni died and left everything to you, you became her chief target."

"I don't believe in that crap," Angel cried. "I mean, she couldn't have made all this happen by mixing up some, I don't know, some concoction of newts' eyes and pussy willow and a strand of my hair and a fingernail clipping and whatnot, could she?"

His three visitors, New Orleans natives all—like Angel, looked back and forth at one another without saying a word.

"She said most of what Giovanni left you was actually your mother's money, and that given how your mother felt about you, she was sure Philomena would have wanted her to have it instead of you."

"Is that all?" Angel cried. "Let her have it! I don't care about the money."

"That still doesn't solve the crime," Hardin jumped in.

"So then why is this significant?" Angel changed the subject. "Voodoo, shmoodoo. What about the boy?"

Hardin lifted a finger. "Ah, the boy! Madame Orioli says he had absolutely nothing to do with it, but that her curses are broad. She says once she casts them she can't always say exactly where they're going to land or precisely what form they'll take."

"That's not what I mean," Angel interjected. "I mean, do we know who he is, who he's related to, *why he might lie—* things like that?

"Not yet," Hardin winced. And so the two friends and the one eager attorney left with their proverbial tails tucked between their legs. "Back to the drawing board," Angel overheard the ever-original Hardin say as they were walking out.

*

That night, sometime past midnight, Angel lay on his cot just barely awake, hovering between this and that other world, still mulling over the day's bad news (so many sheep to count); but he was also attuned to the unusual silence in and around his cell. Fortunately for him, though, instead of keeping him awake and alert, he was far-enough gone and exhausted to allow the quiet to push him over into sleep.

The next thing he knew something cold had clamped down on and clinched his ankles and wrists, and immediately after that some sort of cloth was stuffed in his mouth. His eyes opened and darted around, and it was then he saw Brice and four other inmates, all of whom he recognized from the yard.

Angel squirmed and tried to scream, but his arms and legs were handcuffed, and his screams, muffled by the rag in his mouth, sounded more like low moans.

Angel then experienced his own weightlessness and watched the ceiling seem to move past overhead as he was carried to the cell door. Once there, he was stood upright and his face was pressed up against two of those cold, iron bars. The men quickly unlocked and then re-locked the handcuffs, so that he was suspended and splayed on the bars of his own cell.

They must have stolen handcuffs from guards, Angel reasoned, *over a period of time*. The guards, where were the guards? And then Angel remembered the unusual silence he had heard earlier in the night and felt a deep, sinking feeling in the pit of his stomach. *They must be in on it, too!*

Next, Angel felt his clothes being ripped away from him, heard the sound of buttons bouncing on the cold, cement floor, the thud of his shoes, and the soft, plush fall of cloth collapsing in a heap; and then the heavy, labored breathing of his captors. Before long, amidst a deafening din of cheering and jeering, one of the men had penetrated him and begun thrusting away.

After a while Angel could no longer tell when one man had stopped and another taken over, or if, in fact, they were still fucking him. He was both all sensation and no sensation whatsoever—acutely sensitive, but also numb. His mind now took him outside the cell, where he imagined—if anyone were watching—it must have looked like some sort of medieval ritual, a feeding frenzy, as the men hovered over and around him like so many crows. What was going on in the minds of his attackers Angel could only imagine, and that he'd rather not do. Instead he would just feel what he felt, experience what he was experiencing—*get through it*. He had no other choice.

*

Several weeks later, having spent a full week recovering in the prison infirmary, Angel lay on his cot in a new, single cell, staring up at the ceiling. With his mind, he had projected the future onto that ceiling and, again with his mind, he could push right through it and rush headlong, out of his cell, out of his particular building, out of the entire prison compound, New Orleans, Louisiana, the United

States of America—if he liked, and into blue, blue sky. Beckoned by that call of release, he projected into a future when he would be a free man, cleared of the ludicrous charges against him, a time when he would look back on and remember the horror of what had happened to him in prison. And he could also see that there, with the proper distance, he would be able to locate in that nightmarish experience a true heaviness, a solidity and closeness to the earth he had never felt before.

Dedications

"The White Gloves" is for Sena Jeter Naslund.
"Negative Capability" is for Frankie Paino.
"Five O'Clock Shadow" is for Martha Corazon.
"Killing Time" is for Steve Bauer
"Forcing Forsythia" is for Lee—who gave me the title,
    and for Sena and Flora.
"The Season of 'We'" is for Kirkby Tittle.

Born and raised in the South, Robin Lippincott has made Boston his home since 1978. A graduate of the Vermont College MFA in Writing Program, his short stories, essays, and book reviews have appeared in *The New York Times Book Review*, *The Literary Review*, *The American Voice*, *Christopher Street*, *The Bloomsbury Review*, *Provincetown Arts*, and many other magazines. He has recently completed a novel, *Mr. Dalloway*.

The Fleur-de-lis Press is named to celebrate the life of
Flora Lee Sims Jeter
(1901-1990).